Paw and Order

The Detective Whiskers Cozy Mystery Series

Book One

Chris Abernathy

This is a work of fiction. Character names and descriptions are the product of the author's imagination. Any resemblance to actual persons or pets, living or dead, is entirely coincidental.

Copyright © 2023 Chris Abernathy

Published by Wright on the Mark, LLC.

All rights reserved. No part of this book may be reproduced in any form, without permission from the author or publisher, except as permitted by U.S. copyright law.

Author's Note

This book is best enjoyed with a cat on your lap. Because if they aren't on your lap, you won't know what they are getting up to.

PREFACE

There comes a time in the life of any ambitious cat when they stop what they're doing and take stock of where life has taken them. I didn't have that luxury. Not at the moment. One false move would spell disaster — for myself and Sheila.

Still, my mind couldn't block out the question of *how have I gotten here?*

"Here" is a moonlit beach where I was surrounded by margarita-influenced ladies trying and failing to hold back their giggles as they stumbled toward an almost certain disaster. Confronting a killer was a job for sober professionals, like myself. Yet, I felt powerless to stop them. The former television queen, crafty elementary school teacher, realtor dressed for the board room, and newly widowed empty nester were determined to do what the local police force seemed incapable of, oblivious to the danger.

What would Fred think? All those years of patiently educating me in the skills and procedures of police detecting to have me doing something as reckless as this? Maybe it was a blessing that he wasn't here to see it, although I could use his help.

A swift breeze from the water rustled the sea oats surrounding us in the shadowed dunes. Moonlight reflected from the rim of the margarita glass one of the ladies refused to leave behind. A muffled scream stopped us all in our tracks as another of the ladies stepped on a jagged shell fragment, barefooted and clutching her stiletto heels to the side of her pristine business suit.

As we drew closer to the killer's lair of deceit, my heart pounded underneath my black and white fur, rattling the shiny badge dangling from my collar.

This is it, Whiskers, I told myself. *Time to prove, to yourself and the rest of the world, that this badge is more than some silly trinket.*

ONE

"Oh, Fred. You really outdid yourself this time."

That's my human, Sheila Mason, talking to a dead man. Not the murder victim—he'd be dead soon enough.

I guess I should introduce myself. I'm Detective Whiskers and I'm a cat. People call me a tuxedo cat because of my handsome black and white fur.

Sheila and I were sitting in front of a wide-open set of French doors, staring across grassy dunes at the waves gently washing up on white sand. She'd been sitting there for an hour, holding a pretty gift box with ribbons and ignoring the boring brown boxes. Most of them were just as full as when the moving truck drove away from our new home—a two-bedroom cottage in the most amazing little beach town, Paradise Cove. The papers inside the gift box had brought us here.

Funny thing about humans. A happy couple can go for hours, even days, barely saying a word to each other, and be perfectly content. They don't need to say it. They know it. But when one of them is gone, the other one can't stop talking to them.

Fred passed away the day we retired. Ever since, it's been "Fred this" and "Fred that" and "Fred, did you see that?"

Don't get me wrong. I'm not complaining. It's nice. Sometimes I swear I think I hear him answer, "Yes, Sheila. Columbo's figured it out now."

They loved to watch murder mysteries together.

The pretty box Sheila held was a gift from Fred. A gift he was bringing to her when he died. Pulling it from the packing box caused all of the memories to flood in, and we were both stuck, frozen in our thoughts.

Fred was Sheila's husband and my partner. Together, he and I had solved hundreds and hundreds of crimes in Colorado. Mostly Fred, if I'm honest, but I helped. Yeah, I did a little field work, chasing down the baddies, but I'm not here to brag about my many courageous adventures. Maybe another time. My main thing was helping him figure it all out. Every night after dinner we'd sit down at his desk in the basement and go over his latest case together. During the day, I'd study the classic cases from other great detectives and amateur sleuths ... Lieutenant Columbo, Jessica Fletcher, Lennie Briscoe. Sheila liked having them on the television while she cooked, cleaned, and worried if the detective she married would come home safely.

She was right. Fred really did outdo himself, buying us this house. I can't wait to get out and explore the town. What I saw from the drive in was really special. Not like other beach towns with big condos and lots of traffic. That's thanks to an unusually strong and large home owners association, I had learned. Paradise Cove was unique—mostly built by one developer many years ago who made sure almost all of the town was part of the association. That way the HOA board was able to keep his original vision of a quiet town. Just enough businesses to meet the needs of the community with younger families on one side of town and the section by the beach reserved exclusively for people fifty-five and older. The public beach, of course, was open to everyone.

I have to admit the beach had always made me think of a very different box from the pretty one Sheila was holding. To me, all that sand just looked like the world's biggest litter box. But that was before I came to Paradise Cove and experienced it for myself. Everything looked so clean and perfect as we rode in on the moving truck. Live oak trees lined the streets with Spanish moss dangling from the limbs. Between houses there were thick hibiscus hedges, azaleas, and other tropical blooms.

Fred and Sheila both dreamed of retiring to Florida. Every summer they came down on vacation and explored the beaches, looking for the perfect place, which turned out to be Paradise Cove. Driving the back roads one day, they stopped here and got a room at the Parrot Eyes Inn. The hotel was showing its age but the town was, well, paradise. They knew this was it and started watching for houses to go on the market. Something small a block or two off the water. But the few listings that showed up were sold before they could even visit. Then, just a few weeks before Fred was set to retire, this cottage was listed 'For Sale by Owner.' It wasn't a block or two off the beach, though. It sits right on the beach near the pier. Fred and Sheila had walked past it many times, wondering if the inside was as inviting as the outside and the view. Thanks to the first picture on the listing, they knew. Absolutely stunning.

Sheila also knew it was out of their price range.

Fred, apparently, didn't know that. That night, while we were supposed to be solving crimes together, he called the seller. And begged.

"This is all I can spend," he told her apologetically. "I'm retiring soon, and Paradise Cove is the only place we want to be. I got a small inheritance in college that I never told my wife about. It's not enough to match your listing price, but it's grown, and with our other savings it's close."

I could hear the woman on the other end of the call. Cats have excellent hearing, despite all of the hair in our ears.

"Well, I don't have any kids to leave it to. It's just me now. And that's more than I will need, honestly. You say you're a police officer?"

"Yes, ma'am. Forty years on the force."

"You've helped a lot of people in that time, I'm sure."

"I've tried my best."

There was a long pause in the conversation. I was watching Fred's face, and it wrinkled up more than the bulldog that used to live down the street. Eventually the woman spoke up again.

"You're really going to live here? You and your wife? Not leave it empty most of the year or try to sell it for a profit?"

"Me, my wife, and Detective Whiskers," he promised. "We will be moving down as soon as we can."

"You're bringing another detective with you?" She sounded confused.

"Well, yes ... but not an ordinary detective. My cat, Whiskers, is my partner in crime fighting."

"Oh, tell me about your Whiskers. I love cats." Her voice had changed now. She seemed happy. Fred held the phone next to my face.

"Say hello, Whiskers."

"Good evening, ma'am. Fred showed me the pictures of your beautiful home. It looks so peaceful," I stated as politely as I possibly could.

Fred took the phone back. "He says he's looking forward to enjoying some fresh seafood."

That's *not* what I said. And Fred knows I prefer donuts, like any other cop. But the lady laughed, so no harm done.

"You're going to love it here," the lady said.

Fred teared up a little. And that was that.

He swore me to secrecy, as if Sheila would understand me anyway. For the next few weeks, our evenings were spent with paperwork, bank transfers, and all the things you do when you're buying a home. His caseload was light now because the police chief didn't want to give him any cases he wouldn't be able to finish. Sheila thought we were still solving crimes. No crime in that, is there?

Fred wrapped up the deed in a pretty box to present to Sheila at his retirement party. Tied some ribbon into a nice bow just like she taught him.

And then he died. Suddenly. No warning. On his way to the party, with the box sitting next to him, unopened, where she had sat a thousand times.

Sheila hadn't been sure what to do. "I don't know if I can move to Florida by myself," she told everyone.

I gotta admit that kinda stung. But I knew what she meant. And that's when I made Fred my promise—wherever he was. I would take care of Sheila and protect her so that she could be safe and, eventually, happy in Paradise Cove. "I'll keep an eye on the neighborhood. I'll use everything you taught me to keep the bad guys away. I won't let anything happen to her."

Eventually it was their kids that convinced her to go ahead with it. They'd moved away years ago and had busy lives. But one look at the pictures of the new house, and they swore she would be seeing them, and the grandkids, often in Florida.

And here we were. Staring out the open doors of a cozy cottage at the most amazing sunset either of us had ever seen. It was time for Sheila to rest and enjoy herself, while I stepped up to keep an eye on things.

"I think we'll call it Sunset Cottage, Whiskers. What do you think?"

"Purrfect," I meowed.

You really outdid yourself this time, Fred.

Two

Ding-dong.

"Oh, who can that be?" Sheila asked, finally taking her eyes off the now-faded sunset and placing the pretty box and ribbon on a shelf. "Surely we've met all the neighbors by now."

There had been a steady stream of visitors throughout the day. Clearly, Paradise Cove didn't get new residents very often and they were all eager to see who had moved in.

A *click, click, click* sound had me on alert before the first ring of the doorbell that morning. It was Becky, a local realtor eager to get the scoop on the listing that she had missed, and the clicking came from her stiletto heels on the front porch. "At least Roger didn't get it, either!" Roger, she said, lived in the house to our right and was her competition. Or at least he seemed to think he was.

He'd moved into town a few months ago but still hadn't managed to snag a single listing in the area. Maybe the pressure of choosing between her next-door neighbor and a more established realtor was too much for the previous owner, and that's why she decided to sell it herself without putting up a sign. "I could've gotten her a lot more," Becky announced, apparently not considering that Sheila wouldn't be living here if she had. "You stole this place."

"My husband *bought* it. He did not steal it." Sheila's eyes narrowed. "He never stole anything in his life."

"You tell her," I meowed. If only she would stand up for herself the way she does for Fred and their kids. I hopped on the countertop, turned away, and lifted my tail up high, giving Becky a perfect view of my one hairless spot. Yeah, we do that on purpose.

"Oh, no, Honey ... I just meant ... oh, never mind me," Becky stuttered. "I'm always sticking my foot in my mouth."

Looking at the spikes of her heels I thought she could use them as toothpicks. As long as her foot is up there anyway, right? Becky dressed to impress, looking more New York or Paris than quiet beach village. She seemed to notice that Sheila wasn't impressed. "Here, I brought you some fruit as a welcome gift." Placing a basket on the kitchen counter, Becky and her heels made a hasty, clicking exit. The door nearly closed before she poked her head back in and said, "I almost forgot. Can you come by the clubhouse tonight at seven? We've planned a little welcome party for you."

The door had barely closed, for real this time, and the clicking faded, when someone knocked on it. This visitor must have coordinated with Becky because she, too, walked in with a basket of groceries. They clearly hadn't coordinated outfits, though. This woman wore high-waisted jeans with a colorful assortment of buttons sewn in various places where buttons had no purpose. Her loose-fitting top had "Julia" embroidered on the chest. In complete contrast to Becky's stilettos, her feet were covered in bright-yellow-and-green canvas sneakers.

"I see you've got some nice fruit already. Can I help you with your unpacking?"

This new arrival came without warning sounds, and as a proud detective it concerned me. Normally I would hear a car pull up or a door slam—and I was on alert in a new neighborhood. I leapt up to the windowsill and glanced out just in time to see Becky pulling away on a golf cart. Another golf cart was parked in front of the house. That explains it. Seems like nobody uses cars around here. Those electric carts are quiet. Sneaky. I'm gonna have to be on my toes.

I plopped down onto the kitchen counter and checked out the new basket. Vegetables and a few fresh herbs. No cat food. Or donuts.

"I don't even know where to start unpacking," Sheila responded. "Thank you so much for the groceries."

"Well, since you've got some food, why don't we start with the kitchen boxes? That way you'll be ready when you work up an appetite."

A very sensible suggestion, which wasn't too surprising, as we soon found out that Julia was a school teacher. Not full-time anymore. She had retired a few years back but stayed involved as a substitute. "I get to work when I want to, and when I don't feel like it, I have a little spending money for my little adventures." It seemed she was always going somewhere, doing something. "Hi, I'm Julia." She pointed at the name on her shirt and laughed. "I guess you figured that out."

Julia stayed for about half an hour, and by the time she left, the kitchen boxes were empty, the cabinets were perfectly organized, and I had gotten a very satisfying belly rub. Sheila seemed just a little more settled as she snacked on an apple from the fruit basket.

Then Tarrie Ann arrived. Wow. What a beauty. Now, I'm not attracted to human women. But beauty like this is undeniable, and Tarrie Ann would make any guy stop and stare. Feline, canine, whatever. You remember the TV show *Gilligan's Island*? Fred and Sheila watched the reruns sometimes. Becky could've been Ginger—expensive clothes and too much makeup. But Tarrie Ann was more like Mary Ann. Stunningly beautiful in an innocent, unassuming way, wearing a light sundress that was captivating without being revealing. Even their names were similar, in case you hadn't noticed, which I'm sure you did. And, as it turns out, Tarrie Ann had been on television herself. It wasn't a detective show so I hadn't paid it any attention, but Sheila remembered it.

"You still look just like you did on TV!" I can usually tell when she's 'stretching the truth,' but it seemed sincere to me.

Tarrie Ann blushed. That was maybe just a little rehearsed. I suspect she's become very experienced at responding politely to compliments. I'm sure she gets her fair share and then some. I mean, I'm a cat and I'm over here drooling like there's a donut in front of me. Which there still isn't. She brought a bottle of tequila and some margarita mix. "Welcome to Florida!"

Sheila glanced at her watch, shrugged, pulled down the blender she and Julia had just put away, and made her first batch of frozen drinks in our new home. Tarrie Ann stepped outside and came back with a couple of beach chairs and an umbrella. They spent the next hour relaxing on the beach, chatting away like old friends. Tequila will do that to humans, I've discovered. I kept watch from the window as several men walked by, often doing double takes in Tarrie Ann's direction. Everybody behaved, so I didn't have to step in.

There was one guy that decided to stick around. He carried a fishing pole onto the pier, cast out his line, and sat back like he planned to be there awhile. He was still there after the sun set and showed no signs of leaving. A large bird walked in his direction until it was just a few feet away, then stopped, watching intently. I'll need to keep an eye on them. And the dog next door. Definitely gonna watch out for him, too.

Eventually Tarrie Ann and Sheila came back inside. Tarrie Ann set the empty margarita glasses on the counter and looked Sheila straight in the eyes. "Don't wash these," she said seriously. "A little housewarming gift from me and the girls. Susi is coming over as soon as you get unpacked."

"Susi?" Sheila looked confused.

"She cleans all of our houses. Wonderful girl and cute as a button," Tarrie Ann said, opening the door and heading out so there could be no argument. "This first one is on us, and I guarantee you'll hire her on the spot."

A few more visitors later and the kitchen was pretty well stocked. Things had settled down for a while, and Sheila eventually opened another packing box. The gift box from Fred was on the top and immediately put an end to the unpacking—which brings us back to where this story began. We had spent an hour staring out at the beach and the sunset, quietly thinking our own thoughts.

Then the doorbell rang again. Sheila took a deep breath, set the box gently on a shelf, made herself smile, and opened the door.

"Hi!"

"Hello there, neighbor! I'm Roger. Rog." Pointing to his right, the opposite side from the house with the dog, the man added, "Next door." Roger was wearing a golf shirt and slacks, with a pair of golfing gloves sticking out of the back pocket. Expensive-looking sunglasses. A smile that was way too big, exposing teeth that were way too white. Behind him, parked sideways and taking up two spaces, was the biggest, fanciest golf cart I had ever seen. It looked more like a convertible limousine than a golf cart, but the shiny set of clubs in the back confirmed what it was. He walked in without waiting for an invitation. I started to make a scene to let him know this was not acceptable, but then I noticed something else. Donuts. He carried a box of glazed donuts in. I decided to give him the benefit of the doubt and see how things played out.

"Looks like you haven't started unpacking yet," he stated authoritatively. "It almost seems like you're not even sure about this place."

Donuts aside, I was not getting good vibes here. Not at all. I walked up and placed myself between Sheila and the man. Very close to the donuts, too, but that was just a happy coincidence.

"I'm not in any rush," Sheila replied.

"Sorry," he said, not sounding sorry. "Your husband leave you to do all the work?"

At this point Sheila broke down crying. I hissed at the man who didn't take his cue to leave. Instead, he walked into the kitchen where he set the donuts on the counter then pulled down a glass and filled it with water. Handing it to her he said, "I didn't mean to upset you. Is it just you, then?"

"My husband was supposed to be with me," Sheila replied, "but he passed away suddenly. It's just me and Whiskers now."

Roger paused his verbal onslaught, but not for long. "That's a bold step, moving all this way by yourself from, what, Colorado, was it? Isn't that where I heard you're from? I'm surprised you didn't stay closer to friends and family."

"I'm surprised you never learned to stay out of other people's business," I hissed. Even though I know it won't be understood, I still feel the need to speak up sometimes. Especially since the donuts were already on the counter and officially ours. "And she's not by herself. I'm here, and you'd better not forget it, mister." Sheila could tell I was as upset as she was and stroked her hand down my back gently.

'Rog' kept going. "Look, I don't want to seem insensitive or anything, but your boxes are still packed. There's no shame in changing your mind. I'm a realtor, and if you want to sell this place, I can get you a lot more than you paid for it. I see all the closing prices, and you guys got a steal."

Sheila started to respond to the 'steal' comment but Roger never left an opening.

"As a matter of fact, I've got a contract right here. I'll pay you twenty percent above what you paid, and I'll even pay for those movers to turn their truck around so you never have to mess with these boxes. Whadya say?"

I was just about to lunge at the guy and use my claws to rip up his contract when a woman walked in the still-open front door.

"Roger! Leave our new neighbor alone. She hasn't even gotten to her welcome party yet!" The newcomer was tall, thin, and domineering in comfortable but conservative clothes. "And your monstrosity of a golf cart is parked improperly. Go out and fix it right now, or I'll issue a fine first thing tomorrow morning."

Roger hurried outside, taking with him the contract.

"Hello, Sheila. I'm Nancy. President of the HOA," the lady said, sticking out her right hand. "Thought I'd come give you a ride to the clubhouse for your party."

"Oh, the party!" Sheila jumped up from where she had been sitting. "I haven't prepared anything to take!" She rushed into the kitchen and started looking through the baskets on the counter. I stared at the donuts, willing her not to take them away.

"Don't worry about that," Nancy said. "It's *your* welcome party. You aren't expected to bring anything."

But Sheila had always prided herself on being prepared and courteous. "I can't show up empty-handed to my very first event in my new home. Would a small appetizer be okay?" she asked Nancy timidly. Sheila pulled a big pineapple from the center of the fruit basket along with a couple of tomatoes, red onions, and a handful of cilantro from the basket of veggies. "Now, where did we put the knives?"

Pulling open a few drawers, she located her favorite Santoku chopping knife. It was an expensive one Fred had bought for her, complete with her initials engraved on the blade. Slicing the pineapple down the middle from top to bottom, she opened up the fruit and hollowed out each side.

Then she cut the extracted fruit into chunks and chopped up the onion, tomatoes, and cilantro. After stirring them all together she placed the mixture back into the hollowed-out pineapple, creating a delicious-looking, to humans anyway, and elegant pineapple salsa. Purrfect for a Florida party. That's my Sheila!

"OH! I don't have any tortilla chips!"

Sheila panicked. Nancy assured her there would be a bag at the clubhouse.

Roger walked back in, still carrying his contract, but he didn't even get to say a word. Nancy pointed him out the door again. "Our new neighbor is leaving for the party, and you should be, too. Go!"

"If I can just remember where Julia put my trays, we can head over," Sheila said to Nancy.

Sheila's phone played the chorus of the song "I Fought the Law." It was the ringtone her grandson, Freddy, had set up for himself as a joke. "I'll have to call you back, Freddy," she said, sending the call to voicemail.

I decided to take a long overdue nap. After I figured out a way into that donut box.

THREE

Alas, my nap was not to be.

As she placed her pineapple salsa onto a tray, we were all distracted by a huge commotion outside which startled Sheila, causing her to almost drop the tray. She caught it, fortunately, but not without paying a price. Her right hand bumped up against the knife, giving her a small cut.

The dog was outside behind the house next door, running and barking like crazy. It was easy to see what had its attention. The man who had been fishing at the pier all afternoon was pulling in a catch. The dog wanted that fish.

Sheila had spent the last four decades as a dedicated mother, grandmother, and wife, always taking care of the people around her, so she instinctively opened the side door from the kitchen and stepped outside to try to stop the dog. I wasn't about to let her face this beast alone, so I walked out with her. That was possibly not the best move. Apparently, Sheila's voice and the scent of a previously unknown cat was enough to momentarily distract the dog from the fisherman and his catch. It ran in our direction.

Realizing the danger this created for Sheila and remembering that I had vowed to protect her at all costs, I, of course, took it upon myself to draw the dog away from her. I ran as fast as I could to a live oak tree between the two houses and scampered up into the branches. I bravely stayed there in the hope that the dog would sit by the tree trunk until its human could take it back inside their house. Unfortunately, that didn't work. Seeing me safely perched high in the branches, and probably recognizing how dangerous I was with my sharp claws that held tightly to the tree, the dog took off after the fish again.

What followed was a crazy blur of fur, fish, and blood. I'm a very sharp-eyed cat, when I'm not napping—which I had hoped to be—but even I couldn't make out exactly how it all went down. All I can say for sure is that the fisherman's hand was bleeding and the fish was leaving the scene quickly in the dog's possession. Then Nancy came outside and ran toward the injured man. Another man, apparently the owner of the house the dog escaped from, also ran from his house yelling, "Buster," which I assumed was the dog's name. He was trying to run while buttoning up a Tommy Bahama camp shirt with a big blue marlin dancing on the back.

With Sheila, Nancy, and the fisherman at the pier, the neighbor running from his house, and me standing guard in the tree branches, Buster must have decided his clearest path was into our house. Nancy had left the door wide open, so Buster, and the fish, were inside in no time.

The man from next door rushed toward our house, but Buster had come back out and ran past the man toward the pier again, still carrying most of the fish, although some appeared to have fallen away inside. The fisherman, Nancy, and Sheila dodged out of the way as the dog and the man ran onto the pier. The dog was trapped now, with nowhere to go. The man hooked the lead onto his collar and pulled him back home where they were met by an angry Nancy.

"I've warned you, Mitch. HOA rule number twenty-three. Pets must be on a leash at all times when outside the home!"

"He WAS inside, Nancy," Mitch argued. "I don't know how he got out."

Nancy shot back with, "I don't think he opened the door himself, Mitch. And now Jimmy's got a big cut on his hand. This is the last straw. You'd better be at the next meeting because I'm going to make a motion that Buster be banned from the community."

"What about that cat?" Mitch pointed at me. "Are you going to do anything about that? Only here one day and already causing trouble. It's outside, too, which is probably why Buster ran out here. If you banish Buster, I'll make it my mission to get that cat kicked out of here, too!"

Sheila was stunned. She just stood there, her mouth open. The angry man was actually blaming me for what his dog did.

"Wait, Nancy. Hold on, Mitch." The injured fisherman tried to calm things down. "It's not her fault. And Buster didn't bite me. This"—he held up his bleeding hand—"was from my hook. It got caught on me when Buster grabbed the fish."

Nancy wasn't swayed. "Either way, the dog was loose, and it caused an injury. Enough is enough. Come on, Sheila. We'll be late for your party."

Sheila looked at Jimmy, the fisherman. "Are you going to be okay? I'd clean that up for you, but my first-aid kit is probably at the bottom of a box. God knows which one."

"I'll be fine. These things happen when you fish as much as I do. I've got what I need. Go enjoy yourself. I apologize that it seems I won't be able to join you. And for part of my fish ending up in your house. I'll just step inside and get the rest if that's okay." He stepped inside, unzipping his tackle bag.

"What about you ... Mitch, was it?" Sheila couldn't help but be nice, even after someone was rude to her. "I hope you can come. I'd love to meet my new neighbor in a better situation."

Mitch glanced over at Nancy who gave him the stink-eye. "Oh, I'll be there. I need to make sure you and Nancy aren't telling stories about me." He really was not a very nice man. "But you'll have to excuse me for arriving late. I think I need to clean this fish off myself before I go. And make sure Buster is properly secured, of course," he added sarcastically. "Be sure to do the same with your cat."

"Of course," Sheila replied. She turned to Nancy. "I'll just grab my pineapple salsa, if it survived, and be right out."

With Buster safely back inside his house and no longer a threat to Sheila, I hopped down and walked inside. To her relief, the salsa was fine. To my relief, so were the donuts, although they had been knocked down and the box was now open.

Jimmy left with the remains of his fish. Sheila walked out behind him, carrying the tray with the salsa.

"I'll clean things later, Whiskers. Don't wait up for me."

"Don't worry," I meowed. "As soon as I finish my donut, it's nap time!"

Four

I ate a very delicious donut—okay, two donuts—and licked all the sticky glaze from my paws. The house was quiet, and I was really feeling that nap coming on. Where was that box with Fred's things? I liked to nap on his uniform. Sheila complained at first, said I was getting hair on it, but she was cool with it after all. She knew I missed him, too.

I found it in the back bedroom. Purrfect. The quietest and darkest spot in the house with the window curtains closed. Hopping onto the box, I curled up and tucked my head under my front paw. Then I wrapped my tail around my legs into a nice, black and white circle and closed my eyes.

Before I fell asleep, I heard a noise outside. A door opening. Probably just Mitch heading to the party, I thought.

"I won't be too long, Buster. Can you stay out of trouble while I'm at the party? I've got to try and talk some sense into Nancy. Be a good boy, please!"

The door closed. My eyes closed again.

Another noise: a barely audible scratching sound. Any other time I would have gone to investigate, but if you chase every small noise in a new house, you'll never sleep. So, after such a long day, I decided to let it go.

Sleep, beautiful sleep.

The next thing I heard was Sheila walking in the front door and saying goodbye to Nancy.

"Thanks so much for the ride. And everything. I had a wonderful time!"

"Goodnight, Sheila," Nancy responded. "I'll check back in with you on my morning rounds, see if you need anything. And I've got a copy of the HOA rules we can go over together."

President Nancy really takes her HOA duties seriously. As a law-and-order cat, I respect that. She sure put that 'Rog' in his place. And a good thing, too, because I was about to get physical with him before she showed up. No, I have not been declawed, and he would have known it soon enough.

I do wish she hadn't been so hard on Buster. I'm no great defender of dogs, but they're mostly just lovable oafs. His door was open; he took his chance. He's lucky I went to the tree as a distraction instead of showing him my claws. But she's right. He stole the fish from—what was his name? Jimmy?—and caused an injury in the process. It sounds like it's not his first offense, so something needs to be done. Mitch, though. Not a nice guy. He's got to know what his dog is capable of, and leaving the gate open was irresponsible. Nancy can't just ignore it all.

"Whiskers! I'm home," Sheila sang.

I stretched out my legs, hopped down from the box, and walked into the living area of the new house. "Welcome home. How was the party?"

As usual, she misunderstood me. "No, I'm not giving you any more food. I see you've been into the donuts already."

Sheila picked up the donut box, closed the top, and set it on the counter. Looking around, she took in a deep breath. "That dog sure made a mess of things. But it will all still be here in the morning, as will the boxes. At least the moving boys put my bed together before they left."

"The party was lovely," she finally told me as she kicked off her shoes and plopped on the sofa. "I think the whole neighborhood was there. Almost everyone. I guess Jimmy was home taking care of his hand, the poor man. And Mitch never did show up. That was a relief."

Hang on a sec. "Mitch wasn't at the party?" I asked. "I heard him leave. He told Buster he was going there."

"I already told you, Whiskers. Two donuts is more than enough food for tonight. But you should've seen the spread they had at the party. Everybody in Paradise Cove brought something. And they were all so nice. Tarrie Ann made some more margaritas—mango flavored this time, with fresh mango juice! Julia brought a brownie mocha trifle with crushed Heath bars in it. Even that realtor, Becky, put together the most amazing Key lime pie I've ever tasted. The graham cracker crust was perfect, and she said she'd show me how to make it. I wasn't so keen on her this morning, but I think we just got off on the wrong foot. I even saw Evelyn, the lady that owns the hotel we used to stay in, the Parrot Eyes Inn. Her husband has passed, too, and she's not looking too well. But her son was there taking care of her."

Sheila looked as happy as I'd seen her since, well, you know. Fred would be pleased to see how well most of the community was welcoming her. Or maybe it was Tarrie Ann's margaritas. Either way, I was glad to see her happy. She deserved it. And then her smile faded.

"That other realtor was there, too. Roger from next door. Can you believe it? Not only did he have the nerve to show up after being so rude to me earlier, he parked his golf cart sideways again, taking two spaces when he knew everyone was coming to the party. There we were with no place to park. Nancy was so mad. She dropped me off and drove away to find a space wherever she could. When she finally came in, she said she had called and had it towed!" Sheila was smiling again, but a different smile now. A smirky smile. "I don't think Roger even realized what happened. I finally spotted him sitting in the back of the clubhouse by himself. Like he knew he shouldn't be there but wanted to show up just to spite me. I wouldn't sell this house to him for anything. I'm not selling to anybody. I like it here. I told him that, too. He just harrumphed like he didn't care. Nasty man!"

In case you haven't noticed, Sheila gets a little chatty when she's had margaritas. Then she falls asleep. Which she just did on the sofa. I curled up beside her to keep guard—and take myself another nap.

FIVE

Ding-dong.

I swear, our doorbell never rang this much in Colorado.

Sheila paused Detective Monk on the TV and pushed herself up on the sofa, then slid down again as she seemed to feel the after effects of Tarrie Ann's margaritas. Sunlight was shining brightly through the French doors overlooking the beach, which normally would have pleased Sheila immensely. This morning, not so much. She squeezed her eyes shut and pushed herself up again. Buster was barking loudly next door, causing additional wincing each time.

"Sheila?" It was Nancy's voice at the door. "I brought over the HOA rules to go over with you. Hang on. I'll be right back. I'm going to tell Mitch to get his dog under control. Rule number twenty-four. No excessive barking!"

The barking continued, but at least Sheila had a moment to compose herself. She got up and poured a glass of water in the kitchen, then went through most of the cabinets before she found the coffee beans, grinder, and French press. The electric kettle was already plugged in next to the fridge. While the coffee steeped, she changed into some sweats and a T-shirt. The barking had only gotten worse by the time the coffee was ready.

"Sheila? Are you in there?" Nancy was back.

"Come in," Sheila answered. "Can I pour you some coffee?"

Nancy walked inside like she was on a mission. Which it seemed she always was. "Have you seen Mitch this morning?"

"Fortunately, no. I don't think I could deal with him this morning. Between the moving and the margaritas, I feel like I walked into a wall. Do you think we can go over the rules another time?"

"It seems we'll have to," Nancy responded. "I can't find Mitch, and Buster is going crazy. That dog is a handful, but I've never seen him act like this before. We certainly can't have him barking like this all day right here on the beach. Mitch left all his windows open, and there's nothing to block the sound. I'll be getting complaints from everyone."

Sheila walked over to the side window to see for herself. I joined her. Buster was visible just inside the glass doors, but he almost looked lost. He kept looking around, barking, then looking around again. As if he, too, were looking for Mitch and calling out for him.

Sheila pointed to the other end of Mitch's house. "He can't have gone far. His golf cart is still here. Looks like he's got an oil leak," Sheila said.

"He'd better NOT have an oil leak. Rule number seventy-seven. Electric golf carts only. No noisy gasoline engines. At least he put his trash out. The truck will be coming by any minute now. We'd better get yours out there. This is trash day." She hurried out the door. Sheila followed her, so I went, too.

Nancy found our trash can and rolled it to the curb.

Sheila had gone to examine the oil spill from the golf cart, but I could already tell it wasn't oil. This whole scene was about to get *real* ugly.

"Nancy," Sheila said tentatively. "This isn't oil. This is blood. A lot of blood."

A black-and-white golf cart with a 'Paradise Cove Police Department' logo on the hood pulled up. A tall man with a mustache stepped out. He was wearing khaki shorts and a golf shirt with the same police logo on the chest. I stepped up to introduce myself, but he completely ignored me. Maybe he didn't see the badge on my collar.

"Thanks for calling me, Nancy, but don't go getting yerself too worked up over nothing," the man said in a deep Southern accent. He took a quick look at the blood. "There's probably a perfectly normal explanation for what's going on here. Didn't I hear that Jimmy had a run-in with Mitch's dog here yesterday? I bet this is his blood."

Nancy wasn't having it. "No, Chief Anderson, that happened at the pier. And there wasn't this much blood. He wasn't bleeding anymore when we left for the party."

"So, you left him here?" the chief asked. "And Mitch was still here, I take it. Most likely scenario ... He started bleeding again, Mitch drove him to get it looked at, and now Mitch is having a long walk on the beach tryin' to figger out how he's gonna convince you to let him keep his dog."

I was respectfully allowing the police chief to do his job, but it seemed to me that he was doing more avoiding than investigating. Coming up with excuses to not investigate the crime. And I was convinced that a crime had been committed.

I had heard Mitch leave the previous evening. He walked out the door, said goodbye to Buster, and hadn't been seen since. Sheila said he wasn't at the party. His golf cart was still here, and it had blood on and around it. Mitch was attacked and possibly killed, right here. While I slept next door. "Fred, I'm sorry. I already let you down," I thought to myself. "But I'll find out what happened. And whoever the culprit is, I'll make sure they don't hurt Sheila."

Chief Anderson had started walking toward the back of the house. "Will someone shut that dog up?" Sheila and Nancy followed, but I stayed by the golf cart, looking for any clues. I couldn't hear any more of their conversation. Not only was Buster barking, but the garbage truck had pulled up and was reaching its mechanical arm out to pick Mitch's trash can up.

This isn't good, I thought. *There may be clues in there.* I tried to get someone's attention, but between the truck and Buster, it was too loud. The arm closed around the trash can, lifted it high into the air, twisted, and dumped the contents. I stared in horror as Mitch's lifeless body fell with the trash into the back of the truck.

The arm returned the empty trash can to the curb and the truck drove away.

"I'm sure he'll turn up soon," Chief Anderson said, walking back with his right hand pulling Buster by the collar. "When he does, let him know that Buster's at my office and he can bring him home after he pays the fine for violating the noise ordinance. 'Cause I know you'll be fining him again, Nancy."

Mitch won't be paying any more fines, I thought to myself.

Six

The police chief left with Buster riding in the back of the golf cart, still barking. Nancy said she needed to get home, so the HOA rules would have to wait 'til tomorrow. Sheila, acting disappointed—I know when she's acting—promised to keep an eye out for Mitch while she unpacked boxes. She had Nancy's cell number and would alert her the minute he showed up. Which, of course, he wouldn't.

I set off to do some investigating. The number one piece of evidence in a murder investigation is the body, and I'd already seen that disappear in the garbage truck. I needed to find any other evidence before it disappeared, too.

Now, as you may have figured out, I can't talk to humans, even Fred. Well, I do ... but they don't understand a word I say. I'd tell Fred, "Go talk to the electrician that was helping with the remodeling work. I bet he overheard something." And Fred would respond with something like, "Yeah, it is cold down here. I think I'll turn on the space heater." But just because he didn't understand cat talk doesn't mean I couldn't tell him anything. We had a system. When Fred said something important or picked up the picture with the big clue, I'd pat my paw on his hand twice to let him know he was close. It took us a while, but he caught on. And we caught a lot of bad guys.

Sheila never caught on. She thought it was 'cute' that I sat with Fred while he worked. He told her once that I helped, and she laughed. She told him, "If he's helping you, then he needs a badge." The next day he attached a cat-sized police badge to my collar and made it official. 'Detective Whiskers' was etched on the back with a letter from the Chief of Police declaring me an official detective's assistant. Sheila laughed again. Still does sometimes when she looks at it.

But she never realized I was actually helping Fred solve crimes, which was fine by me. Fred knew and I knew. Nobody else needed to. Now, though, it would be good if she understood. If she could know that I was going to take care of her and protect her the way Fred did. I promised him that.

Sheila does *not* understand. I know we're not supposed to play favorites with our humans, but we all do. Fred and I had a connection that was ... special. I've tried communicating with Sheila, but— Okay this part is a little embarrassing. Every time I tap her hand with my

PAW AND ORDER

paw, she thinks I want food or a belly rub. Which, of course, I do. I ALWAYS want food or a belly rub. Or both. But I'm trying to tell her something important, and all of a sudden, she puts those fingernails to work on my belly and I'm gone. Lost. A zombie. It feels sooooo good. Whatever I needed to say is up in smoke, my eyes are closed, and I hear a Karen Carpenter love song in my head.

Don't judge me.

"Whiskers!" Sheila had noticed I wasn't with her anymore. Being in a new place probably worried her, as if an experienced detective like myself would just wander off and get lost. I'd always been an indoor-outdoor cat and had no plans on changing that.

Mitch's house was now closed up. I could probably find a way in if I needed to, but knowing the crime occurred outside, I decided to focus my attention there. Starting at the far side away from our house, I began to explore the perimeter. A small path went toward the beach in one direction or back between some houses, including one with Nancy's golf cart parked in front. The beach seemed like a better getaway route than past the HOA president's house, so I started to walk toward the sound of gentle waves. Before I got far, I heard a meow.

"Hey, man. Got any 'nip?"

The voice came from just off the trail in a patch of sea oats. A calico cat was lying there, stretched out. If he hadn't spoken to me, I'd be pretty sure he was sleeping.

41

"Excuse me?" I asked.

The cat looked up at me slowly as if the only thing he had was time. When his eyes finally focused on me, I saw him look at my collar.

"Woah, Officer. I didn't know you were a ... wait. Are you a ... for real? Can cats be cops, man?"

He had clearly noticed the badge on my collar.

"Detective Whiskers at your service. What was it you wanted again?" I had heard him the first time but decided to have a little fun.

"Naw, man. It don't matter."

"Some 'nip you said? Would that be catnip?"

"Hey, man, ain't nothin' illegal about it. You ain't local, anyway. I can tell. Ain't no vacation cop gonna bust me over a little 'nip."

"I am local, as of yesterday," I informed the hippie cat. "And I will be patrolling this area from now on, so if you're up to anything you shouldn't be, then you'll need to take that elsewhere from now on."

The formerly 'chill' cat suddenly seemed tense and defensive. "Hey, man ... this beach belongs to everybody, man. You might have a house with a nice view, but that don't mean you own the view. I'm just mindin' my own, catchin' a few rays. Ain't no need to make a fuss."

He was right. I had no reason to bust his chops. But I did have an important investigation to get back to, and he could be a witness. "You hang out here much?" I asked.

"What's it to ya, man?" he responded defensively. "Like I said, man, public beach. Ain't no time limit."

There probably were some ordinances about stray animals, and he wasn't wearing a collar. But, again, that wasn't my concern right then. "I'm not looking to cause you any trouble. But there's been some trouble, and maybe you can help. Do you know the man who lives in this house?" I pointed a paw back toward Mitch's house.

The hippie cat paused. He was relaxing some, but I could tell he wasn't sure if he could trust me. I threw him a peace offering. "My human keeps a little catnip around most of the time. Not sure exactly where at the moment because she's still unpacking, but I can probably get you some soon. Will I find you here?" I was probing to see if my hunch was correct and he lived out here in the wild.

"Yeah, man. I'm pretty much always here. Thanks, man. You're a cool cat after all. I'm Zappa. Nice to meet you, man."

I saw my opening and took it. "Nice to meet you, Zappa. Great sunset last night, wasn't it?"

"Oh, yeah, man. Best sunsets in the world on this beach. I never miss 'em. Watched it from right here. Really makes me feel connected with the sky spirit."

Now that I knew for sure he was here, I went for the real information. "Did you happen to see anything suspicious? Maybe close to sunset?"

"Yeah, man. I saw Buster steal that fish from Jimmy. That what you mean? That really sucked, man, 'cause Jimmy probably would've given me some of that fish."

"Jimmy feeds you?" I asked.

Zappa nodded. "Yeah, man. Me and Blue." He looked over toward the pier where a great blue heron was standing at the edge of the water. "He fishes every day, man. Keeps some of what he catches. The rest he gives to us."

I was getting a picture of Zappa's life and, I have to admit, this hippie cat really had it made. Living on a beautiful beach rent free with all the fresh fish he could eat. It's not the life I would choose, but for a laid-back cat like Zappa, it's ideal. But I still hadn't learned anything about Mitch's death.

"What about after the incident with the fish?" I asked. "Did you notice anything maybe up near Buster's house?"

Zappa stretched back out in the sand. "Can't say that I did, man. I saw Jimmy go in, but there's nothing suspicious about that. He probably went in to wash his hand off, right? Since he'd been bleeding, ya know?"

"You're probably right," I told him. "You say Jimmy's here every day, fishing?"

"Not *every* day. But usually. Shows up mid-afternoon, coming down this path, and fishes 'til after sunset."

I thanked Zappa for his help. "Much appreciated. I may see you again this afternoon."

"Yeah, man. Bring that 'nip if you can."

I left Zappa, lying in the sand, warm sunshine on his belly, dreaming of the fish Jimmy would catch for him later. *Good for you, Zappa*, I thought. *Good for you.*

"Whiskers!"

Sheila was outside, yelling for me to come home. Might as well go back in and take a nap. It had been an eventful morning, and I wanted to be rested for when Jimmy showed up this afternoon. According to Sheila he was about the only person in Paradise Cove, other than Mitch, who wasn't at the party when the crime occurred. He had been injured, and had lost a big fish, because Mitch left the door open. And now, thanks to Zappa, I knew that he had gone inside Mitch's house after everyone else left. I now had my lead suspect.

SEVEN

While I was investigating, Sheila had done some unpacking. There really wasn't that much. The house had come mostly furnished and was tastefully decorated with a nice beach theme that fit the view without being over the top. Sheila insisted on keeping the bed that she and Fred had shared. The kitchen items were already put away. Most of the rest was just clothes and memories. The clothes would need to be updated for the beach instead of mountain living. The memories, things like Fred's uniform and their picture albums, would stay just as they were.

"Here, Whiskers, I put Fred's uniform up here for you." She had folded it up and placed it on a shelf in the living area. "You'll have a nice view of the beach, and you can see the living area and the kitchen. Not that you'll have your eyes open much of the time."

Hopping up from a plush chair, I settled on the shelf and looked around. Sheila was right. An excellent vantage point. From the front door to the deck and the beach, I could see practically everything. That included the television which was currently showing Remington Steele—the episode where Remington wakes up beside a murdered man in an Irish movie theater. Fred's uniform smelled nice. She was also correct about me closing my eyes. I enjoyed a nice midday nap.

Ding-dong.

There goes that doorbell again. Lifting my head, I watched Sheila open the door.

"Chief Anderson," she said. "I hope you're here to say that Mitch showed up and everything is fine."

"Unfortunately, no." The chief's tone of voice was much more serious than it had been this morning. "I've come to ask if you remember any other details from last night. We now think something very bad may have happened."

Sheila motioned for the chief to come in, and they both sat down—Sheila on the sofa and Chief Anderson in the plush chair beside me. He reached out and patted my head. Cats hate that, by the way. All of us. "What's this on your collar? Are you a detective yourself?" he asked in the most patronizing way possible. "I hope you won't be sticking your nose into my investigation!"

"I might be sticking my claws into your face if you keep it up!" I replied. He didn't understand what I said, of course, but he got the message clearly enough to pull his arm back away from me.

"My husband was a detective in Colorado," Sheila told him. "Whiskers was his assistant. He always sat with Fred while he worked on cases at home."

The chief smiled. "That's cute, Mrs. Mason. Officer Whiskers, is it then?"

I exposed my claws.

Sheila jumped in quickly. "*Detective* Whiskers, actually. What changed your mind about Mitch?" Sheila brought the conversation back to the business at hand.

"A new piece of evidence." The chief paused as if debating whether to provide more details. He apparently chose not to. "Have you noticed anyone on the path to the beach? I know you can't see much of it from here, but I'm especially interested in anyone who may have been across the street close to Nancy's house."

"I'm not sure which house is Nancy's," Sheila replied. "But I haven't noticed anyone other than those walking on the beach or on golf carts on the street. If it happened during the party then, of course, I wasn't even here, remember? You were there. Mitch insisted he was going, so it must have happened shortly after Nancy and I left."

"I'll figure out a timeline soon enough, Mrs. Mason. No need to jump to any conclusions. I'm sure your late husband would tell you the same thing." Chief

Anderson gave her a somewhat condescending look, which irritated me and seemed to have a similar effect on Sheila.

He was right. Fred would have said the same thing—without the condescension. But the chief didn't know what I knew. I had heard Mitch leave his house and tell Buster he was going to the party. Humans lie to each other all the time, and someone saying that they're going to a party is hardly conclusive. But they rarely lie to their animals, except about three things: bath time, medicine snuck into a piece of bread or cheese, or a trip to the vet. And the chief clearly hadn't seen what I saw when Mitch's body was dumped from the trash can into the garbage truck. I knew for certain he had been killed, most likely as he was leaving for the party. And, thanks to Zappa, I knew Jimmy was the best suspect as he had gone into Mitch's house at about that time. What I did *not* know, and I was extremely curious about, was the new evidence that convinced Chief Anderson there actually was a crime.

"Can I get you something to drink?" Sheila stood up and walked toward the kitchen.

"Thanks, but no, Mrs. Mason. I need to help my officer look for any more evidence, now that we know a serious crime is likely."

The chief's phone dinged, and he took it from his front pocket. A text message from Officer Reid popped up as the phone recognized his face and unlocked.

"Got the pictures. Bagging it now."

Another ding and a picture appeared on the screen. A knife, bloody, lying in the grass beside a small path. I instantly recognized the knife. It had the initials S.M. engraved on the blade.

Chief Anderson returned his phone to his pocket and looked up suspiciously at Sheila as she poured herself some water. "If you think of something, anything, or if you see or hear from Mitch, let me know immediately, please."

"I will, Chief. I hope it turns out to be nothing."

It wouldn't be nothing, I knew. It would turn out to be murder. And as soon as they realized who the knife belonged to, the police would be back with a very different line of questioning. I needed to find Jimmy, quickly, so as Chief Anderson walked out the door, I darted out beside him.

"Whiskers!" Sheila shouted. "Oh, please don't go far. You don't know your way around yet!"

I didn't need to know much to realize where the knife had been found, and by whom. Standing on the path beside Nancy's house was Jimmy, holding his fishing pole and gesturing to a uniformed officer as if to show where he was walking when he discovered the knife. My number one, and really my only, suspect had just given the police a clue that would point their investigation directly at Sheila.

EIGHT

It wouldn't be good to hang around the crime scene while the police were searching. And Jimmy would be on his best behavior while they were around. So, I decided my best course of action was to talk to Zappa again and find out more about Jimmy. I headed around Mitch's house, turned right onto the path, and walked toward the beach, looking left and right into the dunes for Zappa. He wasn't where I had left him earlier, and I didn't see him anywhere else. I guess maybe the police activity had scared him off. As I got past the dunes, though, I did see someone else.

The great blue heron was standing at the water's edge beside the pier. I'd seen her hanging around near Jimmy yesterday, and Zappa had mentioned that Jimmy shared some of his catches with each of them. Maybe she knew something about the man who might be a killer.

"Hi! Hello there! Blue, is it?"

The bird took a few steps away and otherwise ignored me.

"I saw you out here fishing with Jimmy yesterday." I tried to sound as friendly as possible. "That was some crazy scene with Buster, wasn't it?"

Blue slowly turned her long, slender neck slightly in my direction but still didn't fully face me. "That dog stole my dinner" was all she said.

I resisted the urge to remind her that she was a natural-born fishing machine herself. "It was a big one. Zappa told me that Jimmy shares his catches with you."

"Jimmy's a good man. The only one I really trust on this beach."

There was no easy way to approach this, so I just threw it out there. "I'm not so sure about that. I think he might be a killer."

Blue now turned to face me head-on. "That's a lie! Unless you're talking about fish, Jimmy never hurt anybody. Ask Zappa, he'll tell you the same." She glanced down toward the badge on my collar, and her eyes widened. Blue started to spread her impressive wings.

"I was looking for Zappa but can't find him," I hurriedly said, hoping to get something, anything, from Blue before she flew away.

"He's hiding under that driftwood," the bird said. "Too many cops like you hanging around today!" And with that she flapped her wings and lifted into the air.

I turned and spotted a log in the sand that must be where Zappa was hiding.

"Stay back, man," I heard from the log. "I don't need any cop trouble. Those cages at the police station ain't no place for a free cat like me."

"I'm not working with those officers searching the area," I reassured him.

"I don't know about that, but they got one of them K-9 cops, man, and if he sees you he'll be over here harassing both of us.

A K-9 cop was trouble I did not want. I was suddenly as ready as Zappa to get this over with. "I just want to know about Jimmy. You told me you saw him go into the house here last night. The man that lives there has been killed, and I need to figure out what happened before the wrong person gets in trouble."

Zappa's head peeked out of a spot between the log and the sand. "Jimmy didn't do it. You heard Blue. He ain't the type, man."

"Maybe not," I replied, "but all the evidence so far points to him. I was trained to look for someone who had motive, opportunity, and means. Jimmy had opportunity —he was in the area after everyone else left. He had means—he went inside our house by himself to pick up the fish and could have snuck my human's knife into his tackle bag. And he had motive—Mitch's dog attacked him."

Zappa listened intently and appeared very worried. His perfect life as a beach cat was in jeopardy. If Jimmy got locked up, the free fish deal would disappear. "You got it all wrong, man. I know you do. Jimmy wouldn't hurt nobody."

"Then help me figure it out," I replied. "If he's innocent, he's got nothing to worry about, right?"

"I already told you everything I know, man."

I suspected that was true. Zappa didn't strike me as the most observant cat. What was my next move? I was one step ahead of the local police, but they would catch up fast. While searching the crime scene, they would certainly look inside the trash can and see blood stains from where the body had apparently been all night. It wouldn't take long to figure out the garbage truck had collected it.

"How do I get to the city dump?" I asked Zappa.

"Man, that's a long way," he answered. "You'll need to take the GCE."

"The GCE?"

"Yeah, man. The GCE. Golf Cart Express. These people go everywhere on their golf carts. And that space where the golf clubs are supposed to go? It's almost always empty. Just hop on the back and take a ride."

Great. My witness was a habitual stowaway. But it wasn't a half-bad idea. "How do you know where they're going?" I asked.

"Just pay attention, man. You're a cop. Ain't you supposed to be observant and stuff?"

Getting lectured by a stowaway hippie was not improving my mood. But I needed all the help I could get to save Sheila. "I just arrived in town yesterday. Help me out a little."

"Okay, man. Listen to me. It's mail time. The highlight of the day for most of these people. Hop on any golf cart that's leaving a house. They'll be going to the mail boxes at the clubhouse, aka Grand Central Station. From there you transfer onto one of the single seaters. All the houses close to the beach here have fancy carts with two rows of seats. The houses at the back of the neighborhood have older carts with just one seat. You want the oldest looking cart you can find. That's the one that will get you closest to the dump. There's only one road out of town. Follow it until the smell of the beach is replaced by something much less pleasant. From there, just follow your nose, man."

I had to admit that Zappa made sense, in a crazy, 'I can't believe I'm about to do this' kinda way. But Sheila was sure to be accused of murder and Fred wasn't around to help her anymore. It was up to me. Time to check out the local public transportation and see if I can find Mitch's body.

"Hey, wait up, man. What happened to that 'nip?" Zappa called out as I started walking back to the path.

"Not today. But I appreciate the help. I'll come back with some when I can," I told him.

If Sheila doesn't get arrested, I thought to myself.

NINE

Zappa was none too pleased to find out he'd have to wait for his catnip. If I didn't change my mind. I'm a very lucky cat and I don't mind sharing some of my good fortune, but if this 'GCE' didn't work out ... I was already starting to regret this course of action, but I certainly didn't want to walk all the way to the dump, and I had to stay ahead of the police in case they figured out whom the murder weapon belonged to and got tunnel vision. Fred always said a lot of lazy cops did that. Chief Anderson didn't strike me as the most diligent cop.

It did seem that Zappa was correct about the rush to the mailboxes. Several golf carts were pulling out of driveways and I hopped on the back of a nice red one with a large man behind the wheel. I picked the wrong one, it seemed, as the driver stopped to visit with everyone he passed. All the talk was about Mitch's disappearance.

"Afternoon, Denise. Have you seen the police searching near Nancy's place?"

"Yes. Horrible scene. Maybe it's all a mistake and he'll show up soon."

"I saw them questioning Jimmy. You think he did something?"

"Don't be ridiculous, Phil. Jimmy wouldn't hurt anyone," Denise answered, appearing shocked at the mere suggestion. That seemed to be the consensus, that Jimmy couldn't have done it, but my training told me to ignore opinions and look at facts. And the facts pointed at the fisherman.

We eventually arrived at the clubhouse, where it seemed half of the neighborhood was hanging around the mailboxes, gossiping. Roger had apparently freed his fancy cart from the impound lot. He was standing next to it, surrounded by several residents. "I sure hope Mitch is okay," he said. But before you go thinking the ugly man had grown a heart, don't. "He just signed a contract to sell me his house. I can close the deal with or without him, but it would be a lot easier with!" The obnoxious man laughed.

"Got your ride back, I see," Phil said, either admiring Roger's vehicle or wondering how much money he had blown on it. It was hard to tell if he was jealous or playing with Roger. "Looks like you've damaged your seat, though."

Roger looked at the seat of his cart and saw what Phil was talking about. There was a rip on the driver's side about two inches long. Roger's face went red. "That ... must have happened when they towed it. They'll be buying me a new seat." He sat down behind the steering wheel and took off, almost bumping into an eighty-year-old lady driving about two miles an hour. "Out of my way, June!" he called as she came to as sudden a stop as is possible for someone driving so slowly.

Phil walked over to June to check on her. She seemed out of breath from the incident, but that could have just been normal for a woman of her age. Fortunately, there were at least three people with portable oxygen concentrator machines and masks on their carts. The whole scene clearly irritated Phil. He spotted the cart with the police logo riding by and flagged it down.

"Chief! That idiot, Roger, almost ran over June here. Go get him and write him a ticket for reckless driving. He really is a menace on that monstrosity!"

"No time for traffic violations, Phil," the chief blurted out. "I'm trying to track down a murderer!"

All of the talk around the mailboxes stopped and everyone stared at the chief, jaws dropped and eyes wide open.

"I didn't say that!" The chief tried to take back his revelation.

Phil raised an eyebrow. "I believe you did."

"I mean, I did, but I shouldn't have," the chief stuttered out loudly. "We don't know anything yet. Stop your gossiping and go home, everybody." He leaned in toward Phil and quietly stated, "We found more blood. In the trash can. I'm headed to the dump to see if ..."

"... if the body got carried away by the garbage truck this morning," Phil completed the thought for him.

Good news, bad news. The good news was that I had a ride all the way to the dump. I hopped down from Randy's cart and discretely found my way onto the back of the police cart. The bad news was that I wouldn't be alone out there. The police had caught up. Almost. They probably still didn't know what I knew about Jimmy going into Mitch's house after everyone else left for the party, or that he had been inside our house where he could have stolen the knife. Hopefully they weren't yet sure where the knife came from. With Sheila's initials on it, and with the look Chief Anderson had given her, they clearly already had their suspicions.

Chief Anderson nodded at Phil, looked around, and pulled his fingers across his mouth as if zipping it closed. Phil repeated the motion. As soon as the police cart drove away, I saw Phil huddled together with several people. Secrets didn't last long in Paradise Cove.

TEN

You can't turn on any TV show about police without seeing some human guiding a dog around while it noses its way toward the suspect. Every police department has at least one K-9 officer. Ever see a police department with a cat? Me neither. After all the cases I helped Fred solve it never even once occurred to him that maybe he should bring me to work in an official capacity. I got a badge on my collar and a letter from the chief, and I appreciated that, but it would have been nice to be part of the bigger team. To walk through the halls and hear, "Good morning, Detective Whiskers."

People think that dogs get the jobs because of their noses. They're supposed to be super sniffers, right? And compared to humans they are. But that's not the real reason. The real reason is because dogs will do what you tell them to do. A hearty "Good boy!" and a treat is all you need to get a dog to follow instructions. They're so easy.

Cats? Yeah, no. We're gonna do what we're gonna do. We have our pride. Unless you pull out that laser pointer. That's just not playing fair. I don't know why we can't resist chasing the little red dot, but it's magic. Some alien technology that shouldn't exist on Earth.

But, back to the noses. If noses were the reason dogs got to wear uniforms and be official officers, then it would be a complete farce because we cats are superior smellers. A human nose has about five million olfactory receptors, which sounds like a lot. Kudos to you humans. But cats, even with our much smaller, cuter noses, have 200 million receptors. Our real sniffer super power, though, is our *dual scent mechanism*. I know. It IS very cool.

I'm not gonna get all technical on you. You can research it if you like, but the basic gist is this ... Cats have two organs that work together to detect and identify smells. Working together, they give us a unique ability to detect a smell from across a football field and recognize that smell with an accuracy that dogs can only drool over. Think you're gonna open that bag of kibbles on the other end of the house and surprise us? You got another think coming.

None of this information is new to me. It's frustrated me since the very first case I worked on with Fred. But it was never more infuriating than during the ride to the dump with Chief Anderson. Here I was, badge and all, hiding on the back of his police-logo-covered golf cart while, if I were a dog, I'd be riding up front as the rest of the team waited for me to arrive and lead the search. Life ain't fair. Fred told me that a hundred times, and he proved it by dying the day he retired. But I needed to get over myself and focus on my one and only purpose: saving Sheila from being railroaded for Mitch's murder.

The moment they knew it was Sheila's knife, and I was certain that they would know because of her initials engraved on it and because Jimmy would tell them, they would start looking at the whole case through blinders pointed straight at her. As I considered this, I suddenly realized that was exactly what I was doing with Jimmy. He had motive, means, and opportunity, so he was definitely a suspect, but I had to keep my eyes open to other possibilities as well. And my nose ... which was not happy with me at this point. The smell of the dump was rancid and overpowering before it even came into view. As we pulled up to where the truck had been dumping today's garbage, it became almost too much to bear. But bear it I would to save Sheila.

The old cart came to a stop, and I looked down at the mud beneath. The smell was only half the battle. This nasty stuff was going to get all over my handsome, black and white fur coat, and you know how we cats clean ourselves, right? Not the most dignified thing we do, I have to admit, but that's why we are so careful about where we walk. The K-9 officer that Zappa warned me about was bounding through puddles without a care. I shuddered at the thought.

Eventually, I took a deep breath and hopped down from my clean perch on the cart.

"I've let him smell a dirty shirt we pulled from the victim's laundry room," the officer holding the K-9's lead told the chief. "He's trying to pick up the scent, but it won't be easy out here."

"It's not easy for any of us," Chief Anderson muttered. More loudly, he added, "None of us want to be out here any longer than necessary. Let's get to it."

All eyes were on the dog, so I went the opposite direction to start my own search. I didn't need a shirt—I'd smelled the victim himself as he was unceremoniously dumped into the back of the truck a few hours ago. I fought the urge to shut out smells and took a small sniff of the air. Nothing definitive, but maybe ... I inhaled more deeply. Oh, God it was awful. But I caught the scent. I was sure this time. I padded off as gingerly as I could through the freshly dumped garbage.

Garbage is garbage, wherever you are. There were more mango pits and pineapple rinds here than in Colorado, but mostly the contents of the trash were what I had experienced investigating in dumpsters back home. The big difference was the weather. The hot, humid air along the Gulf Coast amplified everything and made the smells stick in my nose. It was all so overwhelming, I wondered if I would be able to finish the job.

Glancing toward the K-9 officer, I was certain he was headed in the wrong direction. The humans followed, squinting their eyes and holding their noses. They lifted their feet high and tried to put them down in dry spots. Not paying enough attention to my own footsteps, I felt my right front paw slip on something disgusting and looked down. A large chunk of a fish. Eww. How those alley cats ate this rotten stuff was beyond me. But beside the fish was what I had been searching for. It must have been the fish that Buster and Jimmy had fought over yesterday, thrown away in the same garbage can as Mitch's dead body, because a human arm was sticking up right beside it.

I had found the body. Now I just had to find any clues that might be on or near it. Some papers were scattered over the torso, so I pawed them away to get a better look. It was Mitch, alright. I recognized his blue-and-white Tommy Bahama camp shirt. The marlin on the back was shredded with three holes where, apparently, the knife had been thrust in, out, in, out, in, and out one more time. Blood covered the bottom half of the shirt.

The size of the cuts was consistent with Sheila's knife that had been found, or planted, on the trail. Another piece of evidence they would use against her. Nothing else I could see on the body showed me anything of interest. Except ... the papers I had moved. They were blood stained so parts were unreadable, but I noticed a signature line with Mitch's name and the word 'seller' typed below it. It had not been signed. Another line nearby was mostly unreadable. It had been signed with a signature that couldn't have been read in the best of circumstances. The text below the line started with 'R' and 'o' then faded into the blood stains. R. O.—Roger? I pushed through the stack and found the page with a number one in the corner. The top of the page read 'Real Estate Sales Contract.'

Outside the clubhouse, by the mailboxes, Roger had been telling everyone that Mitch had agreed to sell him his house. But Mitch hadn't signed this contract. It had been thrown away. That could be nothing. Or it could be a clue.

The K-9 officer barked, and I could tell he was now closer than when I looked over earlier. He may have finally caught the scent. I needed to hurry.

I pawed through everything in the area quickly. Another sheet of paper caught my eye. It had the Homeowners Association of Paradise Cove logo at the top. Scanning the text that was still legible I saw 'third offense,' 'final warning,' 'dog running loose,' and 'loud barking.' It was signed by Nancy. Nancy had told Mitch that Buster getting loose yesterday was the 'last straw.' Clearly there was a problem between the two of them. Enough to kill over? Probably not, but it warranted some investigating.

The barking was getting closer. Not much time left before I would be chased out of the area and the police would take away all the evidence. Could I find anything else first? There was a bill from a cell phone company, a few junk mail advertisements, and a handwritten note. The note said ...

I need to talk to you before you do anything. It's not what you think. We can sort this all out. Jimmy

"I think he's close, sir!" The voice of the officer holding the K-9's lead was just a few yards away. Time to go. I looked up to see if I could still get away without being noticed.

Chief Anderson replied, "He'd better be! We've been all over this stupid dump. We could have found the body faster *without* that dumb dog." He scanned the area, and I could see his eyes meet mine. "What the ... I know that cat. Is he disturbing my crime scene? Get out of there. Shoo! Shoo!" He waved his arms wildly.

Too late for a clean getaway. Well, that was off the table as soon as I set foot in this filth. I had hoped to go unnoticed, but now, with that blown, my pride got the better of me. I walked straight past the K-9 and said quietly, "All yours, Officer." The dog cocked his head sideways. He stared at me and my collar with that confused look that dogs have perfected. That's one thing they can do better than cats.

Eleven

By this time, I was ready for another nap and the back of the chief's golf cart looked like a very inviting spot, other than the smell of rotting garbage that surrounded me. And the fact that I needed to get back home to Sheila. She would be very worried about me by now, and I was very worried that the police might fix their sights on her really soon. Now that they had a body, it was definitely a murder investigation, and they would be anxious to get someone in custody.

Should I start walking home or wait for a ride? I was pretty sure I could find my way back, but it would take a while. No telling how long the police would be out here digging up evidence. I didn't have to ponder the question for long as I saw the K-9 officer and his handler coming my way. I jumped onto the rear wheel of the cart and peeked out from under the frame. The name on the man's uniform read 'Officer Reid.'

"Let's go home, Officer Kojak. Your job is done. Finally." The K-9's handler seemed unhappy. "The chief was none too pleased that a cat found the body before you did. Didn't make me look good, that's for sure. Or smell good," he added, sniffing his arm.

"Well, it's not exactly a rose garden out here, as you noticed." Officer Kojak pouted. "How am I supposed to sniff out one piece of rotting meat in the middle of hundreds of them?"

"No, you don't get a treat! Find the evidence faster next time if you want a treat!"

It's good to know I'm not the only one who is completely misunderstood by humans.

"Wait!" The K-9 barked. He stopped and sniffed. Uh-oh. He must have smelled me. "That cat is here!"

"Stop messing around, Kojak. Get in the truck." The handler pulled on the lead and directed the K-9 toward an actual truck—not a golf cart. The bed of the truck had a cage installed, and he led Kojak into it then closed the cage door and walked around to get in the front.

This was my chance. The others might be out here forever, but this truck was headed back now and I was going be on it. I crept out from the cart, snuck over to the back of the truck, leapt onto the back bumper, and then jumped into the bed, right beside the cage. Kojak went crazy, barking at me, telling his handler that they had a stowaway. But even if the man looked, he wouldn't see me. I was completely hidden from the view of anyone up front.

"Calm down and enjoy the ride," I said to Kojak. "And don't let them give you any grief about earlier. You did your job. It's not your fault I did it faster."

"Who are you?" Kojak barked angrily.

"Detective Whiskers," I answered. "Happy to assist with the investigation."

"We don't need any assistance. And that's not a real badge, you know?"

That put the hair up on my back. I hissed at the arrogant oaf. "It's as real as any badge you have!" I retorted.

"Not so, kitty cat." He knew he had hit me where it hurt and was enjoying his moment. "I trained for this job. Six months. Graduated top of my class."

"Oh yeah? I worked with the best detective in Colorado for six years. He taught me more than you could possibly know."

"Well, where's your super detective now?" Kojak asked loudly.

I shut down. The arch in my back drooped slowly until I found myself lying on the truck bed, coiled up and trying desperately to hold back tears. It wasn't until this moment that I realized how much I missed Fred. Yeah, it hit me like a truck when his chief told us what happened. The freak accident, hit by an actual truck while on his way to his retirement party at O'Malley's Pub. But I hadn't had a chance to process it all. Sheila and I were both still in shock when they buried him. Once the kids talked Sheila into moving into the house he had bought, it was easy to stay distracted sorting through things ... what to bring, what to leave behind. And then we got down here and, before the boxes were unpacked, there was a murder. The biggest case I'd ever faced because Sheila could be accused, and I had to solve it without Fred. Where's my super detective now? Not here. And it hurt more than I could say. At that moment, I couldn't say anything. I was frozen.

"Hey ... hey ... I didn't mean to ... Are you okay?" Kojak, even with his limited powers of observation, could see he had hit a very sensitive nerve and was trying to be nice. "Something happen to your detective?"

I didn't respond. I couldn't have if I wanted to, which I didn't.

"I didn't mean it about your badge. I'm sure you earned it. You just caught me off guard, ya know? It's my first murder investigation. The first for everyone in the department. Even the chief. We haven't had any of those for a long time, if ever, in Paradise Cove, and Officer Reid is mad at me because you showed us up." He paused for a moment. "How did you get there before us?"

Kojak's question brought me back to reality. I needed to grieve for Fred, but now wasn't the time. I had to honor him by protecting Sheila and solving this case. And, as much as it pained me to admit it, this dog might be able to help.

"I saw, and smelled, the victim before he left the crime scene. I was there when his body was dumped from the trash can into the garbage truck."

Kojak's eyes were wide open. "You witnessed it?"

"Yep. Everybody else was too distracted by Buster's barking. That's the victim's dog."

"Yeah, I met Buster." Kojak's tone was sad now. "They've got him in a cage at the station. He doesn't know what's happened, but he knows something is wrong with his human because he could smell him nearby but he wouldn't answer."

"You haven't told him?" I asked.

"I didn't know anything before we left to search after the knife was found."

"About that knife ..." I wasn't sure how much I should say or if I could trust the K-9 officer. Dogs, though, for all their faults, were trustworthy. "Have they found out anything from it?"

Kojak must have been having similar thoughts, wondering if he could trust me. I guess he decided he could. "One officer to another, confidentially, they found a set of prints. Only from one person, and they haven't found a match yet. And there are initials engraved on the blade."

"Any idea where it came from?" I asked cautiously.

"The chief hasn't said, but he seems to have a hunch. Some guy named Jimmy spotted it beside the path when he was walking down to the beach early this afternoon. That's all anybody seems to know about it."

I decided I needed to trust Kojak. "If I tell you what I know will you help me keep an innocent person from getting set up?"

He looked at me with that confused look again. "How much do you know?"

"Not enough," I answered honestly. And then I caught him up to speed. Told him that the knife belonged to Sheila but there's no way she killed Mitch because she was at the party. Gave him the names of everyone I knew, including the victim, who I had seen go into the house or might have been able to sneak in and take it while Buster was causing a scene. I shared my suspicions about Jimmy, including the note I saw at the dump along with the contract Mitch hadn't signed and the 'last straw' warning from Nancy.

Kojak was amazed at what I had pieced together. "This Jimmy character sounds like the best suspect," he said.

"He had motive, means, and opportunity," I confirmed.

"I take back what I said about your badge not being real," Kojak stated. "You are a real detective after all."

"I'd better be," I told him. "Sheila's depending on me. And I'm counting on you to help any way you can."

"I'll do my best, Detective Whiskers. Officer Kojak is on the case!" He stood straight with his nose pointed slightly up.

Take it down a notch, I thought to myself. Dogs take themselves so seriously, until somebody throws a stick.

We were just arriving at the police station. "How do I get to Grand Central Station from here?" I asked. He gave me the confused look again. "The HOA clubhouse," I clarified.

TWELVE

Using Kojak's directions, I easily found the clubhouse where I hoped to get another ride on the GCE. It wasn't nearly as crowded as it had been at mail time, but I spotted a couple walking toward one of the fancier golf carts and, remembering the advice from Zappa, concluded they would likely be headed to a house by the beach. That should get me close to home where I could, hopefully, take a long overdue nap. I carefully snuck onto the back.

"Todd, did you ... have an accident?" the woman asked the man accusingly.

"I was going to ask you the same thing, Margo," he replied.

The woman made a gagging sound. "Something smells horrid. You need to talk to Nancy and let her know. We can't have Paradise Cove smelling like the city dump!"

Fortunately, it never occurred to the offended couple that the smell could be coming from somewhere on their golf cart. And, not to be petty, but they didn't exactly smell like a can of Fancy Feast themselves. The beach came into sight, another beautiful sunset taking shape. The cart turned onto the street I recognized as ours and I spotted Nancy walking down her driveway, possibly to enjoy the view, but she wasn't going to make it undisturbed. The couple stopped to complain about the smell, and I hopped off. Home was just across the street.

The front door, as expected, was closed, so I decided to check the back. I walked around the side of the house, glancing over at the house next door surrounded by crime scene tape. *Poor Buster*, I thought. What would happen to him with Mitch gone? I looked ahead at the beach and pier. Jimmy was out there fishing again. I thought maybe I should observe him for a while and see if he did anything suspicious. My attention was quickly drawn back to our house where it appeared a party was happening on the deck facing the beach. Sheila was refilling a margarita glass for Tarrie Ann who was lying out in a swimsuit and coverup on one of the chaise lounges. Julia, wearing a cotton sundress with a large cutout of a parrot sewn on the front, and Becky, decked out in a full business suit with heels even higher than before, sat side by side on the outdoor sofa with their own margaritas half full. Sheila set the empty pitcher on a small table and sat down in a lounge chair. They were all laughing about something I must have just missed. I tried not to disturb them as I quietly padded my way to the open French doors, but the smell of the dump drew Becky's attention.

"Is that smell coming from next door?" she asked. They all sniffed and looked in my direction.

"Whiskers! There you are!" Sheila exclaimed. "I've been worried sick about you."

"I can tell," I responded sarcastically.

"Where on Earth have you been to get all covered in filth like that?"

I moved toward the door.

"Oh, no you don't!" Sheila got up and grabbed me, holding me as far away as her arms could stretch. "Susi's been in there cleaning. All the sand and dust the movers brought in, and the mess from that fish, is gone now, and I'm not about to let you smell the house up. You're getting a bath, mister! Julia, would you mind? I know we just unpacked the cat shampoo. I think I put it under the sink."

I was under no illusions about my condition, and I certainly wasn't excited about cleaning myself the usual way this time. As much as I hated getting a bath, it seemed a necessary evil at this point. But did it really have to be in front of all these ladies? Was a cat not allowed any privacy these days?

"Found it!" Julia shouted from the kitchen. She hurried out with the bottle. Becky, quickly clicking across the deck in her heels, had located the hose and turned it on. Tarrie Ann just sat on the chaise lounge watching and giggling. Sheila held me in place on the deck while Becky sprayed water on me, squatting down as far as her ridiculous heels and tight skirt would allow and trying not to get her fancy outfit wet. Instinctually, I struggled. I wanted to be clean, but I couldn't help myself when getting wet. Julia, after spending decades in school classrooms, was unfazed by the chaos and mess. She poured shampoo into her hand, worked it into a lather, and started rubbing it into my long, soiled hair. I shook my body, sending Becky running.

I would never admit this if you told Sheila, but it felt nice. It also felt a little naughty, if I'm honest. A strange lady rubbing me down while others watched and giggled. I'm not exactly sure what all feelings I experienced, but I am sure that I won't be describing them here. I just relaxed the best I could and let the ladies have their way with me. What choice did I have, right?

Tarrie Ann finally stopped giggling long enough to retrieve a towel from the closet inside and help Sheila dry my fur. The moment she let me go, I took off, running inside and rubbing myself on the living room rug. Once I felt I was as dry as I could get, I hopped onto the perch where Sheila had set up Fred's uniform and got settled in for a nap. These dreams could get interesting.

The doors were still open to the deck and I could hear the ladies laughing and chatting. It kept me from falling sound asleep, but it was good to hear Sheila laugh. There hadn't been much of that since Fred passed. He had done well with his final surprise. Not only had he bought her a beautiful cottage on their favorite beach, he had somehow managed to drop her in the middle of what seemed like a great group of new friends.

And a murderer, I reminded myself. Somebody here in Paradise Cove had killed Mitch, dumped his body in a trash can, and dropped the murder weapon—Sheila's knife—where it would surely be found.

"Should I mix up another pitcher of margaritas?" Sheila asked the group.

"The answer to that question is always yes!" Tarrie Ann responded. Everyone laughed again as Sheila got up and walked inside.

"The mix is all gone, but I've got some limes in here with the groceries you all brought me—thank you again. I'll make this round fresh." Sheila started rummaging through drawers. "Now where did I put my good knife?"

Uh-oh. Sheila was about to admit to these women that her knife was missing while everyone in Paradise Cove knew that a knife had been used to kill Mitch. I know what I said about them, and I hoped they would support Sheila, but they didn't know someone was setting her up. I was certain that Jimmy finding the knife was no accident, whether he put it there himself or not, and the police would jump to conclusions. At the very least they would check Sheila's fingerprints. If the murderer had been smart enough to wear gloves, then the one set of prints they found would be hers. Her knife, her prints, her neighbor dead. It was all circumstantial, but people had been convicted on less evidence plenty of times.

Sheila had stopped rummaging and poked her head back outdoors. "I can't find my good knife. You don't think Susi could have ..."

"Absolutely not!" Julia responded before Sheila could even finish the thought. "Susi cleans all of our houses and nothing has ever gone missing."

"Well, I've got a drawer full of socks that are missing their partners," Tarrie Ann joked.

"Don't be silly, Tarrie Ann," Becky laughed. "You've never worn socks in your life!" She turned to Sheila. "When did you last use it?"

"I guess it was when I made the pineapple salsa last night for the party. Right before the dog got loose next door."

"Right before Mitch was stabbed," Julia added ominously.

All the laughter stopped.

Sheila looked horrified. "You don't think he could've been killed with my knife, do you?"

They all looked at each other. "It's possible," Julia said, "but let's not get ahead of ourselves. Just because you can't find a knife in a house you just moved into doesn't mean it's the murder weapon, if he even was murdered. We don't know that for sure yet. I bet it'll show up. Did you look in the dishwasher?"

"Yes," Sheila answered. "It's empty. Susi put everything away."

Becky spoke up in an authoritative and calming voice. "Well, you haven't had time to get everything organized, and today was her first day cleaning for you so she wouldn't know where to put it. It could be in any drawer or who knows where."

"You're probably right," Sheila said, but her voice had lost all of the joy it held just moments ago. "I'm suddenly feeling very tired from all of the unpacking. Perhaps we should save the next pitcher for another night."

"Say no more, Sheila," Tarrie Ann said, picking up the glasses and empty pitcher. She walked inside and placed them in the dishwasher. "We'll leave you to rest and talk in the morning when our heads are clear."

"But not too early in the morning," Julia joked. "Not all of us are immune to the effects of tequila like you, Tarrie Ann!"

Everyone laughed again. Not as loudly as earlier, but they didn't seem too worried. I was. I did know Mitch's fate. And they'd find out soon. As I'd observed at the clubhouse a few hours ago, news travels fast in Paradise Cove. Chief Anderson, already suspicious because of the initials, would hear about Sheila's missing knife. The evidence against her was piling up fast.

Thirteen

Becky, Julia, and Tarrie Ann had left and the house was quiet—not even a murder mystery on TV. The clicking of Becky's heels had faded, and only the sound of the gentle waves on the beach came through the open door to the deck. Sheila was outside, trying to relax in the chaise lounge, but her constant shifting told me that she wasn't succeeding. The quiet scratching sound I heard the previous night was back. This time I decided to investigate, but as I jumped down, I heard another noise. Sand rustling outside. With a murderer on the loose, I wasn't about to let anyone sneak up on Sheila.

"Hello there, neighbor." A sugary-sweet greeting from Roger. He had apparently walked over from his house next door.

Sheila jumped in her seat. "Oh! You startled me," she said, sounding annoyed.

"Must be your guilty conscience," Roger replied.

I stepped in between them and said, "Watch your mouth!" but he knocked me out of the way with his leg and stared at me, daring me to do something about it.

"Don't you hurt Whiskers! Sheila yelled. "I haven't got a clue what you're talking about. I'm not guilty of anything." Her voice cracked as she said it.

Roger just grinned an evil smirk. "You might have the girls fooled, but not me. I heard your little act, pretending not to know where your knife went. The way I figure it, you know the chief will figure out it was yours so you're lining up witnesses to say you were clueless. You're probably lining up some other stooge to take the fall. Don't even deny it."

"You need to leave, Roger." The crack in Sheila's voice was gone now. She may be scared, but she wasn't about to be bullied.

"I'll leave as soon as you agree to sell me this house and leave town." He handed her a set of papers. "All you have to do is sign your name, take your money, and go away. Funny, isn't it? Paradise Cove hasn't had a serious crime like this in years. All of a sudden, less than a day after you move in, your neighbor just happens to get stabbed with your knife."

Sheila raised her voice. "I already told you, ROGER, I'm not selling you this house and I'm not going anywhere." Smart girl. She was making sure that if anyone was nearby, they would not only hear the argument but also

Roger's name. "And you know I didn't do it. You were at the party."

"I was at the party," he replied. "I got there early. But I didn't see you until everyone else was there. You and Nancy showed up after the parking lot was full, remember? You had my cart towed away. The last two people to arrive, it seems. Maybe you did it together. I've never trusted that busybody. And I understand your husband was a cop. I bet he taught you all kinds of tricks to get away with murder."

That did it. I was about to pounce on this creep and shred his face with my claws until Sheila told me not to.

"Stop it, Whiskers. This man isn't worth it." She turned back to Roger. "My Fred was a good man. An honest officer of the law. He taught me how to get away from people who might hurt me, not to get away with any crime, much less murder. Now, I asked you to leave."

Roger stood his ground, but he kept an eye on me. He knew he'd better watch his step. "And I asked you to sell me this house. I asked you nicely, but now I'm telling you. If you don't sign a sales contract by tomorrow morning, I'll go to Chief Anderson and tell him to compare your fingerprints with the ones on that knife. You and I both know they'll match yours. And then it'll be too late." He turned to walk away, then looked back at Sheila. The evil smirk had returned. "Sweet dreams!"

Sheila walked inside, and I followed her. She closed the door, went to the kitchen, opened the dishwasher, and looked at the margarita pitcher. It was upside down and every drop had gone. "Fred, why aren't you here?" she cried softly. "What should I do?"

I rubbed myself gently against her leg. "I'm here, Sheila. Fred prepared me to deal with this. I won't let anything happen to you. I promise."

"Oh, Whiskers, are you okay? I bet you're starving after being out all afternoon, God knows where. Let's get you some kibbles."

I understand why Fred loved Sheila so much. Even now she wants to take care of me. I must catch the killer.

Fourteen

Sheila and I were up for the sunrise the next morning, although she wasn't enjoying it like she normally would. The after-effects of the margaritas prevented her from watching the bright light reveal itself. If not for her worried mind, she likely would have slept in. I certainly would have, and I was already considering my first nap of the day. Sitting here on Sheila's lap while we listened to the waves made dozing off a strong possibility, until ...

Ding-dong.

Really? Who rings the doorbell this early in the morning? Nancy, that's who.

"Good morning, Sheila! I'm coming in," the tall woman declared. Although, in truth, she was already in the house. "I noticed you were up and thought this would be a good time to go over the HOA rules. Sorry it's taken so long." She had made her way through the kitchen and living area and was stepping out onto the deck. "Here, I brought you a latte." She handed Sheila a paper cup with a logo that had the name Sea Brews in a circle around a picture of the beach.

"Does one of those rules say anything about barging into other people's houses uninvited?" I asked snarkily.

"Oh, hello, kitty," she purred, reaching out her hand like she wanted me to smell her finger. I don't know why humans always want us to do that, but I obliged. It smelled like BENGAY. "Good morning to you as well."

I walked off and headed for my perch on the shelf, flashing my spot again.

"Hi, Nancy," Sheila responded, trying not to sound as annoyed as I knew she was. She had a hangover and had slept poorly, worried that she would soon be blamed for her neighbor's murder. The HOA rules were not at the top of her very short list of things she cared about this morning. But she knew Nancy wouldn't stop until she'd made sure Sheila was fully aware of when she could and couldn't put up holiday decorations, how they would know whose pet it was that left a 'present' on the sidewalk and how many people were allowed to reside in a home. And the coffee smelled delicious. "I see you've got a binder for me."

"Indeed, I do," Nancy replied much too cheerfully. I got the impression that this would be the highlight of her day, if not her week. Going over the rules, making sure the new neighbor knew what was expected and who was in charge. "You'll notice that each of these tabs makes it easy to find the section you're looking for. This section has information on where, when, and how to make your monthly dues payments and any other charges or assessments. Don't worry, you're all caught up for the first year. We make that part of the closing to ensure all new residents get off on the right foot."

"That's very considerate of you," Sheila said. "I'll be sure to set up a bank draft sometime in the next twelve months."

Nancy nodded. "Much appreciated. You'll be surprised how quickly it comes around. Time flies when you're having fun. It sounded like you were having fun last night."

Goodness. Did all of the neighbors eavesdrop on her conversation with Julia, Becky, and Tarrie Ann last night? And did she also hear about the knife and the conversation with Roger? I thought of the letter I found at the dump, the one where Nancy was giving Mitch his 'final warning.' And the knife was found beside her property. *Should I be putting her up higher on my list of suspects?* I wondered.

Sheila also seemed concerned that Nancy had been listening. "Were we too loud?" she asked.

"No. You were fine. I used an app on my phone to check the decibel level, and you stayed several decibels below the limit."

Sheila laughed. Nancy didn't. The HOA president opened the binder to the tab labeled 'Noise.'

"You'll see that the noise limits vary based on time of day. We expect everyone to respect the peace throughout the day but especially after the sun goes down. Tarrie Ann has been known to test the limits, but you were fine last night."

"What about the 'Pets' tab?" Sheila asked. I detected a hint of mischief in her voice. "Do I need to have Whiskers come back down and look at his rules?"

If Nancy realized that she was being mocked, she didn't show it. "You, of course, are responsible for your pet's behavior. So go over the rules with him however you choose. I noticed that you allow him to roam the neighborhood."

"Is that a problem?" Now Sheila seemed concerned, and I was, too. Surely, they didn't expect me to stay in the house. "I haven't installed a pet door yet, but I'm planning to."

Nancy took a deep breath and sighed loudly. "There is some debate on that particular topic. The rule says that pets must be on a leash when outside. There has been a general feeling that cats pose no risk to safety and are therefore in a separate category. I've been persuaded so far to not push the issue, against my better judgement." She looked almost embarrassed. "I'm assembling a committee to look over the bylaws for anything that needs clarifying or updating. Frankly, they were poorly written a very long time ago, and it's way past due." She looked at me sternly. "Of course, any animal—cat, dog, whatever—that attacks a resident can no longer stay in Paradise Cove."

So, Roger may have been goading me into attacking him last night, hoping to get me kicked out so that Sheila might leave, too. It's a good thing she stopped me, or he might be getting his way.

"What will happen to Buster?" Sheila asked. She had a big heart for all animals.

"Buster already had a history of causing trouble," Nancy stated matter-of-factly. "With Mitch gone, I suppose the police are in contact with a relative, if they can find one. But he won't be able to stay here. The board will ask Jimmy to make a statement about the attack, and then he will be officially banned from Paradise Cove."

Poor Buster hadn't attacked Jimmy. He just went after a fish. But it seemed to be a moot point anyway.

Nancy continued through the binder, going tab by tab, explaining all the HOA rules such as parking designations, occupancy limits, landscaping requirements, and such. "Short term rentals, of course, are not allowed. Only the Parrot Eyes Inn can rent to tourists. They have an exemption just for their one building," she finished, finally, and closed the binder.

"Any questions?"

"No, I think you covered it all." "I Fought the Law" began playing again from Sheila's phone. "That'll be my grandson. I forgot to call him back."

"I'll leave you to it, then." Nancy stood up and pushed the binder toward Sheila. "Just one other thing," she said. "The elections are coming up soon. I'd appreciate your vote. President of the HOA is a thankless job, but I like to think that I've accomplished some good things in my time. But there's more to do. Not everyone appreciates my ... thoroughness. I hope that you do."

"I'll have to think it over," Sheila responded.

"Of course. Have a pleasant day."

Sheila answered her phone. "Freddy, how is my favorite grandson? Oh, yes, life on the beach is just perfect. When are you coming to visit?"

Their calls could last an hour. Freddy loved his grandmother, and she thought he hung the moon. He was the oldest of the grandkids, in college and planning to be a great detective just like his grandfather. She probably should have told him about the murder. I guess she didn't want him to worry. I settled in for a nap.

FIFTEEN

"Now what shall we do, Whiskers?"

Sheila had showered and prepared us each breakfast. Fancy Feast for me, scrambled eggs and greasy bacon for her. I was ready for a nap, but Sheila seemed anxious to get out and begin exploring her new home. Of course, she knew it well from their visits, but I guess things looked different when you're a 'local.'

"Everything is unpacked and in place, the house is clean, YOU are clean ..." She looked at me accusingly. "I still have no idea how you got so filthy yesterday."

"You don't want to know," I answered.

"Yes, this is a new dress, thank you for noticing."

And there it was again, the doorbell that wouldn't stop. *Ding-dong. This better not be Tarrie Ann with another round of margaritas already*, I thought to myself.

It wasn't. Unfortunately.

"Chief Anderson. Come in. Can I get you a cup of coffee?"

"Thank you, Mrs. Mason, but no. I'm afraid this isn't a social call." He stepped inside and pulled out his phone. "Can you identify this knife for me?" he asked, showing her the picture I had seen earlier.

"That looks like my Santoku knife," she responded cautiously. "I just noticed last night that it had gone missing." She put her hand to her mouth. "Is ... is that blood?"

"I'm afraid it is. We believe it's your former neighbor's blood. I'm going to have to ask you to come to the station with me for a few questions and to get a sample of your fingerprints."

"I don't know what I can tell you," Sheila said. "I used it to cut up a pineapple the other night ..."

"The night Mitch was killed?" Chief Anderson asked.

Sheila paused, getting more visibly nervous. "Yes. That night. I left it on the counter because we were already late for the party after the incident with Buster and Jimmy. Susi cleaned up yesterday, and when I looked for the knife last night it was gone."

"We'll go through it all at the station, Mrs. Mason. I need to get your statement on the record. About the knife and about the argument you had with the victim shortly before he was killed. You might want to bring your toothbrush in case the fingerprints on the weapon match yours."

"You know they will, Chief Anderson. I just told you I used it to cut the pineapple. And we didn't have any argument."

"You're telling me he did not threaten to have your cat kicked out of the community?" the chief asked directly. "I know how much ladies like you love your cats. You probably would have had to pack up and move yourself."

Sheila was too stunned to answer.

"Like I said, you might want to bring your toothbrush. Maybe a few other personal items."

This is what I had been afraid of. The chief had his first suspect in what was, according to Kojak, his first murder investigation. And Sheila didn't exactly have deep ties to the community yet. He wasn't going to take any chances that she might disappear. Not that it would be easy. She didn't even have a golf cart yet. For my part, I knew better than to make a scene. It would only make matters worse. I stayed out of the way.

Sheila had gathered up a few items in a bag and was about to leave with the chief when she suddenly remembered me. "What about Whiskers?"

"I'm glad you reminded me," the chief answered. "Better bring him, too. We'll keep him safe at the station."

I considered running through the open door, and I could have, but I needed to be there for Sheila as long as I could. I let her pick me up, and we rode with the chief on his cart to the station. But once we were there, we were separated. The chief escorted Sheila in the front door. Officer Reid carried me around the building to a structure out back full of cages. He lifted the badge on my collar and read the back.

"*Detective* Whiskers, eh?" he said with a laugh. "I think I'll add impersonating a police officer to your charges. The chief already wanted you for interfering with his investigation."

"I'm more of a policeman than you are!" I snarled at him.

"What's that? You demand a phone call? Good luck with that, kitty cat!"

I scratched his arm.

"Ow! Assaulting a police officer! I'll show you! I've got just the right cage for you."

Leaning down, the officer opened the door to a cage, set me inside, and closed the door. It smelled like dog. And it sounded like dog. A voice I recognized was barking like crazy. In the cage to my right was Buster. To my left was a much larger, nicer cage. Inside it was Kojak, silently staring at me. The officer left, laughing.

Sixteen

"Cut it out, Buster. Haven't you ever seen a cat before?" Kojak bared his teeth to show he meant business.

Buster stopped barking.

"Kojak," I said, "I trusted you." I turned away.

"What?" The K-9 officer seemed confused and hurt.

"You know what. I told you the knife belonged to my human, and the next morning your boss takes her in for questioning. He knows it was hers. How did that happen?"

"Hey ... that wasn't me. I told you. I can't talk to them. I couldn't have told them if I wanted to."

I needed to blame somebody, and Kojak was the only possible source that was nearby. But I believed him. Even with Fred I would have had a hard time getting across that kind of information. I didn't think this dog would be smarter about it than me. So, who told the chief? Did Roger decide not to wait?

"Sorry. I'm just upset. I need your help," I said.

"I'm not sure what I can do," Kojak answered. "I'm locked in, just like you are. When my handler is doing paperwork, he puts me in here. And apparently there's a lot of paperwork when you have a dead body and multiple crime scenes."

"Who told Chief Anderson that the knife belonged to Sheila?" I asked.

"Dunno. Right after we arrived this morning, he got a call. As soon as he hung up, he left. Then he came back with you and your human. That's all I know."

I ran down the list of possibilities in my mind. Obviously, Roger was at the top of the list. He had threatened to call the police last night. But he wanted Sheila to sell him her house and said he was giving her until today. Why would he call this early if he thought he might get his way? Susi had cleaned the house, including the dirty dishes, but she had never seen the knife so how would she know if it was missing? I hadn't met her yet, but the ladies said she was trustworthy. The ladies. Becky, Julia, and Tarrie Ann all knew about it. Would one of them go behind Sheila's back? I didn't want to think that any of them was a fake friend but they had just met Sheila.

Did anybody else know? Possibly. Roger overheard the conversation, so he might not be the only one. Nancy had been listening—and measuring the sound with an app on her phone. How creepy is that? If she did hear it, then she was just the type to call the chief, although she probably wouldn't have waited until the morning. And she was on my list of suspects now that I knew about her problems with Mitch and Buster.

What about my number one suspect, Jimmy? I had seen him fishing at the pier when I got home from the dump. Zappa said he usually stayed past sunset. He could have been eavesdropping.

Of course, whoever killed Mitch already knew who the knife belonged to because they had obviously taken it from Sheila's house. Why did they do that? Was it just taking advantage of an opportunity when they saw the door open and everybody distracted? Or did they use Sheila's knife on purpose to make her look guilty? Either way, they wouldn't have taken it unless they planned to use it so Mitch's murder had to be premeditated. At the very least they were planning to confront him. It didn't just happen in the heat of passion over a sudden argument. And they wouldn't have left it in such an easy-to-find spot unless they wanted it to be found, wanted Sheila to be blamed.

I considered the possibility of a confrontation that had gotten out of hand, but that was unlikely. I would have heard it. I heard Mitch say goodbye to Buster. I would have heard him talking to anyone else.

The only logical conclusion was that someone knew they wanted to kill Mitch. They stole Sheila's knife, hid outside Mitch's house, covered his mouth as he was getting into his golf cart, stabbed him in the back three times, dumped his dead body into the trash can, and placed the knife on the path beside Nancy's house. And it was probably the killer who called the chief about the knife. But how did they explain to him that they knew? They must have waited until they had a way to explain how they knew. Sheila's conversations with the ladies and Roger gave them what they needed to close the net on Sheila.

One more thing was certain now. The killer had been inside our house before the murder and had been in or near our house again last night, either as a guest or snooping around where they could hear what was said. Sheila was in great danger. She might even be safer here at the police station than at home. But I needed to get out. I had to solve this case before it was case closed as far as the police were concerned.

"Kojak. You gotta get me out of here," I pleaded. "I can't solve this case if I'm locked up. And if I don't solve it an innocent person—my human—goes to jail, and a killer —who killed Buster's human—goes free!"

Buster let out a painful moan. He really missed Mitch.

Kojak looked at me. I could tell this was hard for him. He clearly took pride in his work and loved being a K-9 officer. He believed in the law. Helping a prisoner escape went against all of his training and could cost him his job. But he gave me a slight nod, and I knew he would help.

"Buster," he said, "when my handler comes to get me, I need you to cause a distraction."

Buster barked his agreement.

"But wait until I'm out of my cage," he added.

We waited. And we waited. It was probably noon before anything happened, but eventually Officer Reid returned.

"You enjoying your stay, *Detective*?" he said in a condescending tone.

I held my tongue. *Let Kojak do his thing.* I had to trust him. I had no other choice. The handler opened Kojak's cage, attached his lead, and stood up. Suddenly Buster let out a yelp and crashed himself against the door of his cage. Again and again, he ran at the door and hit it with his body as hard as he could. The handler just stared at him, not knowing what was happening or what he should do. Kojak, seeing his opportunity, dipped his long nose down and quietly lifted the latch on my cage, unlocking but not opening the door.

Buster saw Kojak was finished and lay back down in his cage. Officer Reid, happy to not have to deal with the problem, led Kojak away.

"C'mon, boy," he said. "They want us to check out that lady's house. See if you can sniff out anything to show that the victim was there."

That confirmed what I already knew. The police thought they had their killer and now they were looking for anything to help build up their flimsy case. But it also meant I had a ride home. As soon as they walked around the corner, I pushed open the door and walked out of my cage. Silently, I followed Kojak to the truck, and as his handler got in the cab, I hopped up onto the bumper and into the bed. This time Kojak didn't raise a fuss.

I resisted the urge to ask Kojak not to find anything. He had helped me get free. I couldn't ask him not to do his job. Sheila was innocent, and if any evidence had been planted, it would be my job to find out who put it there.

SEVENTEEN

Sheila must have given the police a key to the house. They would have gone in anyway. As Fred used to say, the only difference would be a damaged door and a more suspicious officer. Better to cooperate, especially if you had nothing to hide. Trouble is, I wasn't sure they wouldn't find anything. The killer had been in the house at least once, to steal the knife, so they could have also left something. Based on what Officer Reid said, they would be specifically looking, or more accurately *smelling*, for evidence that Mitch had been inside. If he had been, it was before we moved in. I hadn't left from the time we arrived until after his murder. I would have known. I had gone outside when Buster burst in with the fish, but I could see Mitch the whole time and he never went in.

I tried to sneak in behind Kojak's handler, but he closed the door quickly and I was stuck outside. The French doors that showed off the beach view would give me my best look inside so I jogged around back.

It seemed so wrong, spying on my own house. Watching helplessly as a man and a dog poked around everywhere. Kojak was doing his job well, and by the time he was done he would know this house better than I did. We'd only been living here a couple of days. I'd done a basic check when we arrived, but with the movers barging their way around I thought it best to stay out of their way.

His handler opened doors to all the lower cabinets and let Kojak sniff inside. He was really being thorough. When he got to the trash can he opened it, looked inside, and took something out. Some paper, but I couldn't read it. He put it in an evidence bag, wrote something with a marker, and sealed it. They headed toward the bedrooms.

I wouldn't be able to see them anymore from here, so I was about to reposition myself at a bedroom window when something caught my eye. Kojak and Officer Reid were not alone in the house! Darting across the floor behind them as they left the kitchen was a small mouse. Now I knew what had been causing that scratching sound the last two nights!

The mouse scurried to a tiny crack in the wall beside the couch and disappeared. *It never ceases to amaze me the tight spaces they can squeeze through*, I thought. I made a mental note to take care of the mouse problem at a later date. There were more urgent matters to attend to at the moment.

Moving to the side of the house, I jumped onto the window sill, peeked around the curtains, and watched the two officers, K-9 and human, search the bedrooms. No more evidence bags were pulled out.

It looked as though they were wrapping up their search when I heard the *click, click, click* of stiletto heels on the front porch, followed by the doorbell. I jumped down and peeked around the corner of the house as Officer Reid opened the door.

"What are you doing in Sheila's house?" Becky demanded.

I couldn't see the policeman from where I was, but I could hear him. "I have her permission to search for evidence," he said. I heard the sound of keys jangling like he was holding them up as proof that he belonged there. "But we're all done now, aren't we, Kojak?" The man and dog stepped out the front door. He locked the door and turned to leave.

Becky was upset. "Where is Sheila? What's going on?"

"I can't tell you anything, but I bet you're smart enough to figure it out. A new person moves into town. Their neighbor gets killed. A cop and his K-9 officer search her house." He grinned at her. "If you can't figure it out, then me telling you wouldn't make much difference."

Becky was giving him grief. While he put Kojak in the back of the truck, she kept telling him that they were idiots, investigating the wrong person. The officer ignored her, got in his truck, and drove away.

Becky got on her golf cart and sped away herself, leaving a small amount of rubber as she took off. Her phone was at her ear. "Julia! Get Tarrie Ann and meet me at the police station. Now!"

I was alone now—locked out of the house and not sure what my next move was. At least someone was helping Sheila. I wouldn't want to be Chief Anderson when Becky, Julia, and Tarrie Ann showed up. What could I do now to figure out and prove who the real killer was? Maybe a walk on the beach would help clear my head so I could make sense of it all. I slowly walked toward the soft roar of the waves and saw that I hadn't been the only one spying on the officer while he searched the house. Jimmy, my main suspect, was walking down from a small dune toward the pier.

But was he still my main suspect? Spying on our house while it was being searched certainly didn't make him look innocent. But I guess anybody would be curious if they saw police searching a neighbor's house after a murder. And something about the note I found at the dump didn't quite match up with what I had deduced. He had told Mitch that he wanted to talk. He wrote that something wasn't as it seemed. Everything I knew about the murder made me believe that it happened quickly, without any talking. I was close enough that I would have heard an argument, unless they were whispering, which wasn't out of the question. Maybe. I definitely couldn't rule him out. He was the only suspect that didn't have an alibi. Everyone else was at the party when the crime happened. I decided a little surveillance wouldn't hurt.

Sneaking down to the edge of the dunes, I settled in to watch Jimmy. He cast his fishing line into the water and settled in himself, sitting on a bench built into the pier. Blue flew into view. Holding her majestic wings wide open, she glided down to a spot at the edge of the water close to the pier and stood there.

"Afternoon, Blue!" Jimmy called out.

Blue just stood there, watching, not moving.

The waves made their gentle roar as they slowly crashed on the white sand, one after another after another. The sun was shining. The sand was warm. Some gulls called out in the distance. A cool breeze blew in from the Gulf of Mexico. The name Paradise Cove really fit this place.

Jimmy cried out. I awoke from my catnap. Don't judge me. It's what we do, and I dare say anyone would doze off under these conditions. I looked over to the pier and saw Jimmy struggling with his fishing rod. The curve on the rod told me that whatever he had hooked was impressive. Jimmy took his time, reeling in a little, letting the fish swim, reeling in some more. Eventually he pulled up a fish that looked to be about two feet long.

"Redfish, Blue! You want this one?" Blue was already walking closer to the pier. Jimmy unhooked the fish and placed it on the pier for the grateful bird who hurried over and made a nice lunch out of it. A little further down the dunes I saw Zappa poke his head out. Jimmy laughed. "Don't worry. You'll get the next one." Jimmy prepared his hook again, threw his line out into the water, and settled back on his bench again.

I laid my head back down. It made sense why Zappa and Blue defended him. The generous fisherman didn't seem like your typical stab-a-man-in-the-back killer. And people who take care of animals are rarely bad to people. I needed to think some more about this. I thought for about two seconds before I was napping again on the warm beach. I felt guilty, napping while Sheila was in police custody, but I couldn't figure out anything else to do and the stress had really worn me out.

Eighteen

Zappa got his meal, as promised, and Jimmy kept a couple of fish for himself. Various vacationers and locals came and went, picking up shells and crying out when they got splashed by the water which hadn't yet warmed up enough for swimming at this point in the season. I floated in and out of naps but never saw Jimmy do anything to indicate he was a cold-blooded murderer.

Eventually I heard a familiar voice from the direction of the house. It was Tarrie Ann saying, "You need a margarita!"

Scrambling back over the dunes, I saw Sheila getting off the passenger side of Tarrie Ann's golf cart. The *click, click, click* of Becky's stiletto heels announced her arrival as well. I kept a safe distance from the deadly sharp shoes and met them all at the front door.

"Whiskers!" Sheila was both happy and surprised to see me. "I should have known you would make it back here. Chief Anderson told me you'd gotten out of his cage. How did you do that?"

"I had a little help on the inside," I told her.

"Yes, I imagine you are hungry. Come inside and I'll get you some dinner."

"Speaking of dinner," Becky said, "Julia said she'd pick up some pizzas and be right over."

"She's an angel," Sheila replied. "I'm famished. They offered me a drink and a sandwich at the police station, but I didn't touch it. I was too upset to eat."

That was good to hear. They were probably trying to get a DNA sample, but she didn't bite. Literally.

"You're all angels," she continued. "My guardian angels. Without the three of you, I'd be sitting in a cold cell right now." Sheila tried to keep herself together but couldn't. She broke down crying. "I miss Fred so much," she sobbed.

"Listen, Sheila. I know we've just met, but you're one of us now," Becky said, putting an arm around her and trying to comfort her while making sure no mascara got on her designer suit.

"You're safe at home and we're going to keep it that way," Tarrie Ann added as she pulled out the blender. "Becky and Julia and I have got your back. What on Earth was the chief thinking? He knew you couldn't have done it.

He was at the party. He saw you there. I think he was even flirting with you."

"If anyone can recognize flirting, Tarrie Ann, it's you," Becky stated with a little smirk, before letting go of Sheila and pulling out a tissue. "You're certainly the resident expert!" She started to wipe her suit jacket with the tissue before Tarrie Ann glared at her and motioned toward Sheila. Becky handed Sheila the tissue and got a fresh one to wipe her suit with.

Tarrie Ann took Becky's comment as a compliment. She mixed up the margaritas while Sheila opened up a Fancy Feast for me and told them what had happened. "Someone called this morning and told him that the knife they found was mine."

"Who?" Becky interrupted.

"He didn't say. But he showed me the knife and asked me. I had to tell him that, yes, it was mine. It was awful, looking at my knife and seeing blood all over it. I was fingerprinted and, of course, my fingerprints matched the ones they found. No other prints were on there, he said. They were waiting on forensics to see if the blood matched the victi ... Mitch's, but he seemed certain it would. The poor man."

"We all feel sorry for Mitch," Tarrie Ann said, pouring margarita into the glasses. "But the only thing we can do for him now is catch his killer—which isn't you!"

"I know that. And I hope the chief believes me now, thanks to you girls and Nancy. He wasn't watching me all night and didn't see when I arrived so, as far as he knew, I could have slipped out and come back. But with four reliable witnesses, he had to let me go once the medical examiner confirmed the time of death. Mitch died around the time I arrived. Nancy was with me before then, and you two and Julia never left me alone at the party."

"We wouldn't dare leave a pretty woman like you alone in the middle of all those dirty old men," Julia said, walking in the door with two large pizza boxes and what appeared to be a pair of blown glass shakers. "Red pepper flakes and hand-grated parmesan," she said, smiling and handing the homemade shakers to Sheila. "You'll find out soon enough that you're wanted in this town, and not just by Chief Anderson!"

I didn't care to hear this. And neither did Sheila, I'm relieved to say.

"Oh, I'm not interested in any of that!" she exclaimed.

"You may not be, but I can assure you they are," Tarrie Ann stated. The girls then went down a long list of men to watch out for. Some widowers, some married, one playboy type who never settled down. This may be a retirement community, but there was apparently a lot more action than one might think. Even Becky and Julia were shocked at some of the stories Tarrie Ann told them. "But," she insisted, "they keep their zippers up around me. I may flirt a little ..."

Becky coughed and Julia snorted.

"Okay, more than a little. But that's as far as it goes."

"We still don't know who told the chief it was your knife," Julia said. I was glad to hear her change the subject and get back to the urgent matter of finding Mitch's killer. "There's something bothering me about that."

"What?" asked Sheila.

"How did they know? The caller, I mean. How did this person know that the knife belonged you? I don't think the police have shown it to anyone."

"Which means," Becky blurted, "that whoever made the call might be the killer!"

Way to go girls, I thought. They were starting to connect some dots and make some progress. I couldn't believe the chief missed that. Maybe he didn't but was just keeping his suspicions to himself. I walked over to where Sheila was seated on the couch and sat down in her lap.

"Chief Anderson showed it to me," Sheila noted. "Others in the department would have seen it when they were checking fingerprints and testing the blood. Who else knew?"

"I guess we did, sort of," Julia said. "We didn't see it after it was found, but you told us it was missing so we knew enough to make the call."

"But we didn't!" Becky exclaimed defensively.

Tarrie Ann didn't freak out. "I'm pretty sure Sheila knows it wasn't us."

Sheila nodded. "I wouldn't think that for a second. But ..."

"But what? Becky asked impatiently.

Sheila continued. "Roger overheard us last night. He came over after you all left and threatened to call if I wouldn't sell my house to him."

"That son of a ..." Becky was about to explode. "It's a good thing your knife is gone, or I might take it and kill him with it! Is he so desperate to get listings that he's buying houses so he can sell them?"

"He's buying Mitch's house," Julia said. "Apparently, he told everyone at the clubhouse yesterday that Mitch had signed a contract before he died. Would that even hold up now that he's dead?"

"The contract would still be binding," Becky answered. "It would delay things most likely, and the heirs could challenge it, but they would probably lose."

Sheila had a question. "He wouldn't be able to build a condo or anything like that, would he? Is that what he's after?"

"No," Becky replied. "Overnight accommodations and short-term rentals are against HOA rules, except the Parrot Eyes Inn. They were grandfathered in."

"So, is Roger our suspect now?" Tarrie Ann asked.

"He's certainly *a* suspect," Sheila answered. "But he's not the only person outside of the police who could have known about the knife. Jimmy found it and could have seen it while the mess with the dog was going on."

I wanted to let Sheila know that Jimmy was a prime suspect. They didn't know about him going inside Mitch's house or about the note saying he wanted to talk about something. Some problem that could be worked out. I tapped her hand twice with my paw, like I did with Fred when he was close to a big clue.

"Yes, Whiskers. I'll give you some attention." Sheila reached her hand down to my belly and started scratching softly. Oh, it felt so good. I was powerless. I rolled over on my back, feelings of joy and shame washing over me simultaneously. I sure wished she understood my signal, but her belly scratches were pure heaven. I purred loudly. The ladies giggled. Humiliation and elation mixed together. Karen Carpenter sang in my head. I completely forgot what I was even trying to tell her.

Sheila talked while she scratched. "And Nancy watched me cut the pineapple. The knife was found right beside her house, and you know she was watching. She could have seen it clearly."

Julia jumped back in. "We're overlooking one important thing. The killer, whoever they are, took the knife from here. They already knew whose knife it was before it was found."

"Well, crap," Tarrie Ann said. "Maybe solving crimes and drinking margaritas isn't the best combination."

"I think that's the first time you ever said anything bad about a margarita!" Julia joked.

Everyone laughed.

We weren't any closer to solving the case and catching the killer. At least Sheila was off the hook, for now. I still wanted to know what Kojak and Officer Reid had found in the trash. This might not be over.

NINETEEN

My afternoon on the beach had me rested and ready for fresh excitement tonight. Not that I really expected any, but it would be par for the course. Our first night here someone got murdered next door. Last night Roger had appeared out of nowhere to make a scene.

Sheila hadn't had the luxury of a nap on the beach. The ladies knew she was tired, and even Tarrie Ann didn't suggest a second round of margaritas. They ate pizza, watched another fantastic sunset over the beach, and said goodnight.

"I think I'll take a short stroll on the beach, Whiskers." Sheila hadn't been down to the water since Tarrie Ann first showed up with drinks and chairs. She deserved a quiet walk in the moonlight. I was nervous about her being alone with a killer on the loose, but whoever it was wanted her to get arrested, not killed. I was probably more useful watching the house in case they came back to plant evidence. Plus, I had something else to do.

"Don't go anywhere," she instructed me and went out the door, closing it behind her. I watched as she walked to the water line, stopped for a moment, then walked to her right—away from the pier.

Time to set my mouse trap.

Earlier in the evening, while the ladies were enjoying their pizza, I kept my eyes open for an opportunity. Tarrie Ann provided one when she laughed at a joke while holding a large slice and accidentally dropped some cheese onto the floor. I pounced before anyone noticed. I hid the cheese for later. With the house to myself, I retrieved the mozzarella and placed it in the middle of the floor in the living room. Easy to see and smell from the tiny crack in the baseboard beside the couch.

I jumped up on the couch and settled on the arm where I could ambush anything that came crawling out. I also could see straight ahead to the French doors overlooking the beach so I'd know when Sheila got home. The light on the deck was on.

Unlike this afternoon's attempt at surveillance, there was no warm sunshine and the gentle roar of the waves was mostly muted with the doors closed. I was well-rested, ready, and alert. I remained perfectly still, quiet as a ... No, not quiet as a mouse. Cats were quieter when we wanted to be. Mice made a scratching noise, as I had noted the last couple of evenings. Years of being spoiled by Fancy Feast dinners and belly scratches had softened me, I had to admit, but a deadly hunter still lay inside me, and the instinct had been reawakened in my recent adventures. No mouse stood a chance.

Waiting. Patient. Alert. Frozen like a statue, ready to strike at the first sign of an intruder.

Nothing. For the longest time I didn't hear or see anything. Then ... the scratching sound returned. It was coming from inside the wall, getting closer to the crack I had seen the mouse escape into this afternoon. My hind leg muscles tightened, ready to pounce.

The tiniest nose appeared at the edge of the crack. It wiggled, probably sensing the cheese nearby. And then ...

The sound of footsteps on the wooden deck outside scared the mouse into retreat. Sheila was home at just the wrong time, carrying an armful of shells. I glared out at her, frustrated, then alarmed as I noticed the silhouette of a second body approaching the deck, following several steps behind Sheila! As she opened the door, the stalker came into the light and I saw clearly the face of the man I suspected of killing Mitch. Jimmy was coming up behind her!

"Sheila ..." he said, getting her attention.

"Come inside and close the door!" I meowed loudly.

Sheila turned, surprised, and dropped several of her shells. "Jimmy? You scared me."

"I'm sorry. I didn't mean to," he apologized while helping her pick up the shells. "I saw you walking back from the beach and hoped I could talk to you for a minute."

"Don't!" I said, desperately wishing she could understand me just this once.

"I'm really tired and ready for bed," she told him. "It's been a long day."

Jimmy pressed her. "I know it has been. I saw them searching your house earlier. It's all over the community that you were questioned as a suspect in Mitch's murder."

"I didn't do it!" Sheila said forcefully. "I wasn't even here when it happened."

"I know. I saw you leave. And I'm pretty sure I was the last person to see Mitch alive."

"The last?" Sheila asked.

"Well, the last other than the killer," he clarified. "I didn't do it, either. Can I please come inside?"

On one paw I wanted her to say no, slam the door in his face, and call the police. On another paw, if he wanted to hurt her, he could have done it on the beach, in the dark, without risking being seen or heard on her porch. Mitch's murder had been carefully planned. This wasn't.

I didn't think he meant to harm Sheila, at least right now, and I was very interested in what he had to say.

Sheila thought for a second, walked inside, and held the door open. She offered Jimmy a seat on the couch but he declined.

"I've been fishing all day. Wouldn't want to smell up your nice furniture," he said.

The smell was hard not to notice.

"So why do you think you were the last person to see Mitch alive?" Sheila asked.

"I talked to him after you and Nancy left for the party. I went in his house to clean up my hand and clear up a misunderstanding."

This was getting interesting. Jimmy had just admitted two things that could put him in the crosshairs of Chief Anderson's investigation. He had been alone with the victim, so he had opportunity. And there was a misunderstanding that needed clearing up, so he had motive. I already knew these things, and the chief had probably found the note, but Jimmy didn't know that and the chief likely didn't know Jimmy had been in the house. Would Jimmy admit these things if he really was the killer?

"What kind of misunderstanding?" Sheila asked.

Excellent question, Sheila. Fred would be proud of you, I thought.

"He thought that Nancy was renting out rooms in her house to vacationers," Jimmy told her. "Which isn't true."

"Why on Earth would he think that? Nancy is a stickler for the rules." Sheila was confused, and so was I.

"Yes, she is," Jimmy continued. "And she was going to use the rules to have Buster kicked out of the community. I would have told the board that Buster didn't attack me, he just went after the fish, but she might have succeeded. Buster is an escape artist. He keeps getting loose. Attack or not, this would be the final straw."

"Okay, but what made Mitch think she was renting out rooms?"

"Her house is directly across the street from Mitch's." Jimmy pointed to Nancy's house. "He could see in her window at night. And she's had people staying there. Just not renters."

"Who?"

"Have you met Susi? The housecleaner?" Jimmy asked.

"I have," Sheila answered. "She cleaned here yesterday, and I've hired her to come back once a week. Seems like a really sweet girl."

"She is," Jimmy agreed. "But her family is in a jam. They lost the lease on their apartment and can't move into their new place for another week or so. Susi didn't want anyone to know, but Nancy doesn't miss a thing. She knew something was wrong, got Susi to tell her, and then insisted that they stay at her house."

"I'm impressed. I wouldn't have expected her to do that." She thought about it for a second. "How did you know?"

"I walk past her house after fishing every evening. I saw Susi coming outside with her mother, and she asked me to keep it to myself," Jimmy said. "She was embarrassed, and she didn't want Nancy to get in trouble."

"Why would Nancy get in trouble if she wasn't renting? Just helping somebody?"

"Occupancy limits," Jimmy explained. "Too many people living in a two-bedroom house. I explained the situation to Mitch, but he didn't care. Nancy was being a stickler over Buster and he was going to report her. Not only that, he was going to run against her for HOA president, claiming that Nancy was unfit for office because she didn't follow the same rules she refused to bend for anyone else."

Sheila was shocked. "That's awful. Susi's family would be homeless."

Jimmy nodded his head slowly. "Which means they, and Nancy, had a motive to kill Mitch. And if one of them did it, it's my fault."

"Your fault?" Sheila asked. "Why would it be your fault?"

"When Mitch told me he wouldn't back down, I texted Nancy," Jimmy explained. He asked Sheila, "Did she leave the party at all?"

"No, she ..." Sheila paused. "She had to park her golf cart somewhere away from the clubhouse after she dropped me off because Roger was taking up two spaces! I don't really know how long she was gone. What about Susi's family? Do you know if they were there that night?"

"They were when I left Mitch's. At least some of them. I walked down my normal path beside Nancy's house. The curtains were closed, but I saw lights on and shadows on the curtains."

Sheila and Jimmy stared at each other for what seemed like forever. Eventually Sheila said what they both seemed to be thinking. "The police need to know about this. Even if they didn't do it, Susi and her family might have seen something."

"I know you're right," Jimmy replied. "I hate to cause them any more trouble than they're already dealing with, but I'll go talk to Chief Anderson in the morning. He'll find out soon enough anyway, and I don't want him thinking I hid anything."

Twenty

The next morning, Sheila was in no hurry to wake up. Eventually I let her know that at least one of us could use some breakfast. The weather was still nice, so we went for a quiet stroll on the beach. It was pretty. Blue was enjoying the peaceful view as well but flew away when we got close.

"Oh my gosh!" Sheila said when she saw Blue spread her big wings and fly off. "That's what we used to call those birds, Whiskers. 'Oh my gosh' birds." I had to admit Blue made a big impression.

Sheila picked up a few nice shells to add to the collection she had started last night. "I don't know what I'll do with them," she told me, "but they're too beautiful not to bring home."

"As long as you don't bring back any more that start walking through the house," I said. One of the big ones she brought home earlier had a hermit crab inside of it and went walking along the countertop last night. It woke us up and almost gave me a heart attack when it fell to the floor.

The stroll lasted longer than I think either of us had expected. We both had a lot on our minds, so walking along the beach was a great way to sort out our thoughts. When we got back close to our cottage, we saw three people sitting on the deck. They waved, and soon we could tell it was the girls: Tarrie Ann, Becky, and Julia.

"There you are ... We almost gave up waiting," Tarrie Ann said. "Sandy Scoops has a new ice cream flavor today, and we're going to be the first to try it. Care to join us?"

Sheila didn't take much convincing. She held the door open for me to go back inside, but I didn't. Ice cream isn't my thing, but I wanted to get the scoop all the same. Maybe the girls knew something about the police investigation. They all hopped onto Tarrie Ann's golf cart and I jumped into Sheila's lap. I got to ride up front for once! Tarrie Ann took off, driving faster than Mario Andretti with Becky's heels sticking off the back like miniature jousting poles. Julia sat cross-legged, perfectly balanced and not even bothering to hold on.

I'd seen Sandy Scoops the day we arrived in town. Across the street from the Parrot Eyes Inn. The store itself was very small with just enough room to look at the flavors then enjoy your treats at three picnic tables outside shaded by colorful umbrellas. A sign on the sidewalk read 'New! Pineapple Mango Tango.' I waited outside while the girls went in and ordered. Soon, they were all enjoying their cones, and the owner had even sent out a treat for me. It's nice to be remembered!

All the girls agreed ... the ice cream was delicious. They got quiet as everyone tried to stay ahead of the melting desserts dripping down. A couple of men walked by, smiling at Tarrie Ann. She smiled back and winked at one, drawing a quick elbow from a laughing Julia.

They were getting down to the cones when Jimmy walked up.

"Have you been to see the chief?" Sheila asked.

Jimmy nodded. "I have. Good thing, too, because he was about to look for me. They found a note I left for Mitch near his body at the dump. Chief Anderson was interested in what I wanted to talk to Mitch about. Maybe showing up first will make me look less guilty."

"Did you tell him you'd been in the house that night?"

The girls had been preoccupied by their ice cream, but now they were paying close attention.

"I did," Jimmy answered. "He asked a lot of questions about what I saw and heard. And he wants to talk to you now."

"He already talked to me," Sheila said. "I told him everything."

"Not quite," Jimmy replied. "You didn't tell him about Nancy leaving to park her golf cart after dropping you off."

Sheila looked worried. "Should I go talk to him?"

"I'm sure he'll be in touch real soon." Jimmy sighed. "This whole mess has worn me out. I need to go fishing." He nodded to the ladies and walked off.

All eyes were on Sheila now. Tarrie Ann, Julia, and Becky raised their eyebrows and waited for her to spill the beans.

"Jimmy stopped by last night—almost scared me to death, to be honest," she told them. Sheila shared what she had learned ... About Nancy's guests, Mitch's plan to use them against her, and Jimmy's text to Nancy that night.

Julia spoke up. "So that means there are more potential suspects than we thought."

"You don't think?" Becky asked. "Susi wouldn't kill anyone!"

"I don't believe she would, no," Julia answered. "But we don't know her family. And we all know how much Nosey Nancy loves being president."

"Enough to kill for it?" Tarrie Ann asked incredulously.

Julia shrugged. "Who knows? *Somebody* killed him. And the people in the neighborhood who either weren't at the party or left at some point, are Jimmy, Nancy, and

Susi's family." Everyone wore long faces, in spite of their ice cream, as they thought about the possibilities.

Across the street, a door opened at the Inn and Roger stepped out, followed by a middle-aged man. They crossed at the crosswalk toward the ice cream shop, chatting, then Roger reached in his pocket.

"I gotta take this," he said to the other man. "I'll see you tonight. Come over around seven."

The man walked back to the Inn while Roger walked toward us, talking on his phone while lighting a cigar.

"I'll be home in a few minutes. Just drop it off there. And that seat better be perfect or I'll sue your company and the HOA for damages." He ended the call and placed the phone in his pocket as he walked by, puffing smoke and not even glancing at anyone seated there.

Tarrie Ann sneezed. "What a nasty man," she said, loudly enough that she must have hoped he would hear, but he didn't react. "I can't stand the smell of cigars. They make me sneeze every time."

"Was that Kevin, the son of the Inn owners, he was talking to?" Sheila asked.

Becky nodded. "Yeah. He's a developer from the Miami area. What do you think Roger was complaining about on the phone? Why would he sue the HOA?"

"His beloved golf cart," Julia answered. "Apparently the company that towed it caused a gash on his front seat.

He made a big scene at the clubhouse when someone pointed it out. Almost ran over ..."

Sheila interrupted. "That's not right. The gash on his seat was already there before it got towed. Nancy and I saw it."

"So, he's just blaming them so he doesn't have to pay for it himself!" Julia huffed. "I wish it was him that killed Mitch. Then we could get rid of him. But if he arrived at the party before you, there's no way. We all saw him sitting in that corner until late, like he was just there to spite us."

"Or ..." Sheila said, then got distracted as her phone rang.

"Hello? Yes. I understand. I'll be home in a few minutes." She pressed the screen to hang up and set the phone on the table. "Chief Anderson. He'll be at my house in half an hour."

TWENTY-ONE

Tarrie Ann offered to take Sheila home on her golf cart, but Sheila declined. "I need to walk off that ice cream," she said. Of course, that meant I had to walk as well. I was not consulted on the matter. As we walked across the street, an elderly lady walked out of the Parrot Eyes Inn.

"Sheila! How are you settling in?"

"Oh, hi!" Sheila said, obviously recognizing the woman. "Other than being a suspect in my neighbor's murder, I'm doing great," Sheila replied.

"Good morning," I added, not sure if it was still morning or afternoon now. She hadn't noticed me, then she looked down.

"Your cat is lovely! May I?" The lady looked at Sheila, not me, when she asked the question. That's one thing I don't get about humans. If they want to pet me or another animal, they don't ask our permission. They ask another human. We are the ones being groped. But most of the time it's fine, unless it's kids—and they don't ask. She ran her hand down my back then scratched my cheek.

"You look well, Evelyn."

Evelyn ... Sheila had mentioned her after the party. The owner of the Inn.

"You're kind to say that, but I'm starting to feel as old as this Inn looks. I'm not sure how much longer I can keep it open." Evelyn's excitement at seeing Sheila had faded already. "It needs renovations, as you know, and I think it would take more than I can handle. It might be cheaper to tear it down and start over."

"Your son, Kevin. He's helping you, isn't he?" Sheila asked.

"Oh, yes," Evelyn said. "He's taken over all the book-keeping. He's a huge help, when he's not hanging out with his buddy, Roger. Excuse me ... *Rog*," she said with a touch of drama. "I can't say I care much for that man, but Kevin's far too old for me to choose his friends for him. I guess it's just good that he has someone here he knows from Miami."

Sheila nodded her head understandingly. "Roger is from Miami?"

"Yes, they did some deal together down there. He's in here at the bar every day, probably scheming on some other deal. I guess he bought his house about the same time Kevin came up."

That didn't seem like a coincidence to me. Paradise Cove is such a small place, and very few people seem to know about it. Two people from Miami both decide to move here at the same time? But Roger could have easily learned about it from Kevin, and the charm of the town is hard to miss.

"I was just heading out to get some lunch," Evelyn said. "Would you care to join me?"

Sheila shook her head. "I wish I could. Another time, I promise. Chief Anderson wants to talk to me. He'll be at my house in just a few minutes."

Evelyn looked shocked. "I thought you were joking about being a suspect. Didn't they get that all cleared up?"

"I thought so," Sheila replied. "He knows I was at the party when Mitch was killed. I think he wants to talk about Nancy. I didn't think to mention that she had left for a few minutes."

"Nancy?" Evelyn's shocked expression only grew. "Do they think she did it?"

"Maybe. I don't know. I guess I'll find out more in a few minutes. I'd better go."

Evelyn went off in the direction we had come from, and we continued our walk home. When we got there, the black-and-white golf cart was already out front with

Chief Anderson behind the wheel, talking on his phone.

"Thanks for clearing that up, Nancy," he said. "I may have some more questions, but I need to run now." He ended the call and looked at us. "Are you still interfering in my case, Officer Whiskers?"

"That's *Detective* Whiskers," I responded. "And I do have some information that I think you would find very interesting."

"Okay, I'll give you a belly rub," he replied and reached down.

I moved away. As much as I love a good belly rub, I didn't trust him. I'd escaped from his cages once, and he could be trying to put me back there.

"Why don't we all go inside," Sheila said. I slipped in and sat on the sofa next to Sheila's favorite spot as soon as he opened the door. I wanted to be close. The chief settled into the armchair.

"I had a nice chat with Jimmy this morning," Chief Anderson started. "Turns out he was probably the last person to see Mitch alive. But you already know that."

"The last person other than the killer," Sheila corrected him. "You don't think he did it, do you?"

"I can't rule him out," the chief answered. "He was there after everyone else left for the party. He found the murder weapon and, as you told us in your interview

PAW AND ORDER

before, he was in your house alone so he could have taken it. So, he had means and opportunity. I'm not convinced of his motive, though, unless he's lying to us about what he wanted to discuss with Mitch. It does seem a little bit curious that the last person to see the victim alive was also the person who found the weapon."

"But would he come to you and tell you all this if he was guilty?" Sheila asked.

"He might. We would have found out, anyway. We discovered some evidence that pointed us in that direction already."

The note at the dump. Jimmy mentioned that they had found it. I wondered if they found the other items I saw, and maybe some additional clues.

"What about Nancy," Sheila asked, "and the people ..."

"The people staying at Nancy's house?" The chief completed her thought. "I'll be talking to Susi and her family shortly. I just got off the phone with Nancy, as you may have noticed."

"I should have told you that she left to move her cart," Sheila said apologetically. "I just didn't think about it. I'm not sure how long she was gone. Do you think she killed him to save her position as HOA president?"

"Again, I can't rule out the possibility, especially after seeing the text Jimmy sent her so close to the time of the murder. But I'm not here to talk about Nancy." Chief

Anderson looked sternly at Sheila. He let his statement sink in.

Sheila became defensive. "Are you accusing me? We've already been through this. I was at the party!"

"Were you?" the chief asked, raising an eyebrow. "The whole time?"

"Yes!" she exclaimed.

"The thing is, you no longer have a witness for part of the time. We originally understood that you were with Nancy until the time you walked into the clubhouse, and then you were with your new friends until the party ended and Nancy brought you home. But as Nancy clarified just now, she left to move her golf cart before you walked inside to meet up with the rest. While she was gone, she got the text from Jimmy and called Susi to talk about the living arrangements. That timeline gives her enough time to get back and kill Mitch. But it does the same for you, too. And you're still the only person whose fingerprints are on the murder weapon."

Twenty-Two

Sheila was a wreck. Chief Anderson had stayed for an hour, asking her time and time again about exactly how things had gone down that night.

"Who was in your house after you used the knife?"

"Nancy, Me, Jimmy. And Buster, the dog."

"Did you lock your doors when you left for the party?"

"Yes."

"Was anyone outside to see you go in the clubhouse when you say you did, as soon as Nancy left?"

"No."

"Did the victim threaten to have your cat kicked out of the community?"

"Yes."

"Would that have been devastating to you? Since your husband is gone and the cat is the only friend you have with you?"

"Yes, I would have had to leave myself. I would have sold this place to Roger and gone home."

I kept telling her to stop talking, but she just kept rubbing my belly. I guess she needed a friend more than legal advice, but she was giving the chief everything he needed to make his case against her. Opportunity: she could have had time to walk back and commit the crime. Means: the murder weapon was hers and had her fingerprints on it. Motive: she was scared of being forced to move before she even unpacked our boxes. Scared that she would be leaving behind the last gift Fred ever gave to her.

The chief still had other suspects—Jimmy, Nancy, Susi, and Susi's family—but there was no evidence that Susi had access to the knife before the murder, Jimmy had a reasonable explanation for his actions, and Nancy's motive wasn't very convincing. Sheila was suspect number one again—this time without a solid alibi.

Chief Anderson had left with a warning. "Don't leave town."

"I don't even have a golf cart yet!" Sheila said.

After he was gone, she went straight to her bedroom and lay down. I hopped up on the bed beside her but stayed awake and alert. I was running out of time to solve this case and keep her from being charged with murder.

PAW AND ORDER

The house was quiet. Even in the middle of the day there was very little noise in Paradise Cove. Occasionally, someone said something to a passerby as they rode past on their golf cart.

And then the scratching sound came back. I pounced from the bed and silently strode into the living area, returning to my perch on the arm of the sofa right above the small crack in the wall. Just in time. A tiny pink nose appeared first, sniffing around, then the mouse gingerly stepped out. I let it take a few steps away from the wall, then sprang from above, surprising the trespasser and trapping its tail underneath my right front paw.

"Got you!" I said.

"Let me go!" The mouse was struggling to free itself, but there was no way I was going to lose my grasp.

"This is a private residence," I announced, "and you have not been invited."

"I was here long before you were! I should be kicking you and that human out!"

"That human owns this house. And you are in no position to be arguing, I'd say," I replied smugly.

"Yeah, well ... from what I overheard earlier, you might not be here for long." Now the mouse sounded smug. I liked his chutzpah, but I didn't care at all for the insinuation.

"Sheila did NOT kill that man!" I yelled, then glanced toward the bedroom, hoping I hadn't woken her up.

The mouse stopped struggling and looked straight at me. "I know that. Maybe we can come to an agreement."

"What kind of agreement? What do you know?" Fred had told me that once you got a suspect in custody they would often lie and create any kind of story they could think up to make a deal. But if this mouse really did know something ...

"Your human told that cop there were two people besides her in the house between the time she cut the pineapple and when she left. But there were actually three."

This was huge news, if it was true. "Who else?" I asked.

"Not so fast. I've made a home in this place, and I've done it without bothering anybody. I want a guarantee that you'll let me stay as long as I stay out of sight and don't steal anything that doesn't fall on the floor. That way it's more like I'm cleaning up than trespassing, right?"

I wasn't buying it. But I'd caught this critter once, and I could catch it again. If the information turned out to be false, he'd wish he'd just packed up and left already.

"Okay. Deal—if you're telling the truth. If not, I *will* find you." I glared at him with a look I hoped he would never forget.

"Fine. Shake on it? I'm Roddy, by the way." The mouse held up a tiny foot.

"I'm not lifting my paw off your tail until I know what you know."

"Jeez. Just like a cop. You really don't trust anybody, do you?" Roddy said, not really asking.

"Certainly not you. Spill it. Now."

Roddy took a deep breath. "I was here when that whole mess went down, watching to see who was moving in. When that dog went wild next door, your lady left and the other lady was still inside for a minute. A few minutes after the dog ran in, the guy that smelled like fish came in for a minute."

"I know all that," I told him, frustrated that he was just repeating what I had seen myself.

"But," Roddy stated in a know-it-all manner, "while *you* were *hiding* in the tree, I saw another human walk in the front door, come to the kitchen, and walk back out the front door."

"I wasn't *hiding* in the tree! I was distracting the dog to keep Sheila safe!" I protested.

"Whatever helps you sleep at night, mister," Roddy replied sarcastically. "Are you really gonna let your pride keep you from hearing what I'm saying? I saw someone come in the front door and take the knife everyone is fussing about!"

"Who?"

"The guy who brought the donuts. Thanks for leaving me some, by the way."

Roger. That jerk. He killed Mitch and made it look like Sheila did it so that he could buy both of their houses. But why? And how did he do it while he was at the party? And, most importantly, how could I prove it to Chief Anderson before Sheila went to jail?

Twenty-Three

I kept my promise and let Roddy go. I even let him pick up some crumbs before scampering back into his hole in the wall. If he was lying, it would be his last meal. But I had a feeling he was telling the truth. Roger made sense, other than the alibi. Maybe he had an accomplice?

Sheila napped through the afternoon. Around sunset Julia showed up and rang the doorbell.

"Have you finished it already?" Sheila asked, looking at a small pillow Julia was carrying.

"Oh, it was nothing. Just a little cutting, sewing, and stuffing," she answered, walking over to my shelf. I hadn't noticed before because I'd been busy with Roddy and watching over Sheila, but Fred's uniform was missing. Julia placed the pillow on the shelf where it had been and walked over to me. "I hope you don't mind," she said, scratching my chin. "Sheila thought it was a good idea. I took Fred's pants and made you a nice, soft cushion."

Immediately, I hopped onto the arm of the chair and up to the shelf. I sniffed the pillow. Fred's smell was still there, along with something new. My name embroidered along one edge—'Detective Whiskers.' I poked it with my leg. Soft. I plopped myself on top, moving around in a circle and poking here and there. Eventually I lay down and curled up into a ball. So comfy. It was the next best thing to sitting in Fred's lap.

Julia smiled and turned back to Sheila who quickly wiped away a small tear.

"We've been trying to call you all afternoon," Julia said. "How did it go with Chief Anderson?"

"Sorry ... I had my phone on silent while I took a nap. It did not go well, and I guess I just shut down."

Sheila started to tell Julia about the questioning, but Julia stopped her.

"The other girls are just as anxious to hear this as I am. I'll let them know to come over." She sent two quick text messages and got two quick replies. "Tarrie Ann says to go ahead and make margaritas."

Not more than five minutes later, clicking heels out front told me that Becky had arrived. Tarrie Ann was right behind her. Soon they were all seated on the back porch with drinks in their hands.

"Chief Anderson thinks I killed Mitch," Sheila finally blurted out.

"But he already knows you were with us!" exclaimed Becky. "We've been through this already."

"But," Sheila explained, "when he found out that Nancy dropped me off and left to park her golf cart before I walked into the clubhouse, he decided that I could have snuck away then. There's a hole in my alibi that's really only about five seconds long, but I can't prove how long it is because nobody else saw when Nancy left."

Becky was only getting more upset. She stood up and paced across the deck, the clicking of her heels marking time like a fast waltz and raising everyone's anxiety. "Well then, why isn't he interrogating Nancy since he knows she left?"

"He has talked to her, but it's my knife with my fingerprints on it. And Mitch threatened to get Whiskers kicked out of the community."

Julia interjected, "And if that lazy cop sees an easy path to close the case, he'll take it faster than the last donut. Especially if it means he doesn't have to go head-to-head with Nancy."

"In that case," Tarrie Ann said, "we only have one choice."

We all looked at her, waiting.

"Find the real killer!" she exclaimed.

"It's Roger," I meowed. "Roger did it! Roddy told me."

"Oh, come here, Whiskers. It'll be alright." Sheila picked me up and started rubbing my belly.

I just lay there, helpless to do anything but soak in the sweet euphoria. *Curse you, belly rubs*, I thought. *How can I let Sheila know that Roger came in the house and took the knife?*

Julia did what school teachers do. She started getting the group organized. "Let's go down our list of possible suspects and see if we can figure anything out."

"Jimmy's been at the top of the list," Becky said. "But I just don't believe he did it. If he wanted Mitch gone, he could just file a complaint about Buster attacking him then let Nancy do the rest."

Tarrie Ann agreed. "And he just doesn't seem the type. Now, Nancy loves being HOA president. She would not be happy about Mitch running against her."

Julia nodded. "That's true. But is stabbing someone really her style? She's more the type to use the system to get her way. I don't think Mitch stood a chance against her. And if he did use Susi and her family against Nancy, it would have killed his chances. Sorry, bad choice of words. But, don't you agree? Everybody loves Susi. Helping her out would only make Nancy seem more human and likable."

"I think you're right," Tarrie Ann said. "And I've fixed that problem. I told Susi she could use my spare room.

Between my house and Nancy's, we can keep them all close to each other without breaking the stupid occupancy rules."

"Did you ask what they were doing that night?" Julia asked. "None of us think Susi is a killer, and I doubt she could have put Mitch's body into the trash can by herself. But we don't really know her family, do we?"

Tarrie Ann shook her head. "She couldn't lift him. Someone in her family, maybe, but if one of them is the killer, they're all in on it. Susi told me that they took the opportunity to enjoy the beach while everyone was at the party. As soon as they saw Jimmy walk past, they all walked down together."

"They might have seen the killer!" Sheila exclaimed. "Did you ask if they saw anyone?"

"I did," Tarrie Ann replied. "They were trying not to be seen, so they looked around and didn't see anyone. After Nancy called her, they went back to pack up in case they had to leave."

"But," Becky jumped in, "the killer may have seen them. If someone was hiding, waiting for Mitch to come out, they would have seen them walking down the path beside his house. That might be why the knife was left beside Nancy's house."

"To make it look like they left it there?" asked Julia. "Possibly, but I don't think it would work. Anybody who thought it through enough to steal the knife and to hide the body where the trash truck would take it away would have to be smart enough to not leave the murder weapon outside the house where they were living against the rules. The only motive they would have to kill Mitch would be to keep him from telling on them and getting them kicked out. Leaving the knife on that part of the path would be crazy. No, I think it was put there so Jimmy would find it, but not until after the trash—and Mitch's body—was gone."

"If that's the case," Sheila said, still rubbing my belly, "it would have to be someone who knows Jimmy uses that path and when he uses it. That probably means someone who sees him out there every day."

"Most of us walk on the beach, so that could be just about anybody in town," Tarrie Ann reasoned. "But someone who lives where they can see him from their house would be the most suspicious, and that would be you, Sheila, so I don't know if we want to mention that to anybody."

"I'm already looking too guilty," Sheila agreed. "What about Roger? Can he see the pier from his hou— OUCH!"

That 'ouch' was my fault. I was still mostly helpless with Sheila rubbing my belly, but when she mentioned Roger, I knew I had to get her attention. So, I bit her. A little harder than I meant to. Hey, she never understands when I tap her hand and this was important!

"What was that for, Whiskers?" Sheila asked.

"Roger! Roger did it!" I told her again.

"Ok. I'll put you down." She set me on the floor, and I started pacing, wondering how I could get her to understand.

"The answer is yes," Becky said. She had finally stopped pacing and stared at the house next door. "Roger can see from his house. I was the listing agent when he bought it, so I took pictures of the view."

"Keep going," I told them. "You're on the right track!"

"Quiet down, Whiskers!" Sheila looked at me, annoyed. "This is important." She turned back to the girls. "There's something else I found out about him. Did you know he was friends with Evelyn's son from the Inn? Kevin? And they did real estate deals together in Miami."

Becky shook her head. "He never said anything about that when he bought the house."

Julia leaned in. "Could that explain why Roger is buying up houses? They're trying to do some real estate deal together here? Are they going to build a big condo on the beach?"

"They can't do that," Becky answered. "With his house, Mitch's, and this one, they would have enough room, but the HOA rules don't allow anything bigger than a single-family dwelling this side of Main Street."

Julia leaned back, looking both disappointed and relieved. "Yeah, you said the only exception was the Parrot Eyes Inn, right?"

"Right." Becky drummed her fingers on her temple. "But I can't remember exactly what the exception says. And it's getting to be a very big coincidence with Kevin and Roger doing real estate deals together and keeping quiet about it."

Sheila walked over to the bookshelf and picked out the binder Nancy had left. She found the tab for 'Architectural Guidelines' and started thumbing through it. There were several pages. Everyone leaned in to look.

"There it is," Becky said. "... with the single exception of the business known as the Parrot Eyes Inn, which shall be allowed to maintain or rebuild at the current height of thirty-six feet."

"It doesn't say anything about WHERE!" Sheila exclaimed. "They could tear it down and rebuild on the beach!"

"But only residential buildings are allowed on this side of Main Street," Becky stated.

"The Parrot Eyes Inn is on this side already," Sheila said. "All the other businesses are lined up across the street."

"She's right," Tarrie Ann affirmed. "Did they make another exception in the rules?"

Becky continued thumbing through the binder until she saw what they were looking for. "All areas south of Main Street shall be reserved exclusively for residential single-family dwellings, with the exception of the business known as the Parrot Eyes Inn which shall be allowed to continue as a business providing lodging, food, and drinks to the general public."

Becky was shocked. "Whoever wrote these bylaws was either negligent or sneaky. This section hasn't been updated in decades. I guess nobody ever considered the possibility that they would move the Inn. I don't see anything here that says they can't."

Julia jumped up. "And the only thing left is for them to get rid of Sheila! Roger said he had a contract to buy Mitch's house. With the three properties side by side, they could build a new hotel with a bar on the beach."

"It would be worth millions!" Becky, the realtor, had already done enough of the math to know it would make both Roger and Kevin extremely rich.

"But it would ruin the town," Tarrie Ann replied. "Everything unique about Paradise Cove would be gone."

"And so would I," Sheila added. "Gone to jail for a murder I didn't commit. We have to figure how they did it and find a way to prove it. Roger and Kevin were both at the party, so how could they?"

"I was thinking about that," Julia said. "Do we really know that Roger was there the whole time? When you arrived you saw his golf cart, but did you see him? I once marked a student present because he had left his backpack the previous day. I kept calling on him in class until

I had to turn around because all the kids were laughing."

Sheila's eyes narrowed. "The sneaky jerk! I didn't see him until later and thought it was just because he was in a back corner. He must have parked in two front spaces on purpose, to make sure everyone saw his cart and assumed he was there somewhere. He would have had plenty of time to walk back, kill Mitch, and sneak in the back door. And he was here right before Buster got loose. I bet he opened Mitch's door and waited for Buster to get loose. As soon as we walked outside, he probably snuck back in the front door and stole my knife."

"Exactly!" I yowled. They ignored me.

"I'm calling Chief Anderson," Julia announced.

"But what will you tell him?" Sheila asked. "We can't prove anything."

"Wait," interrupted Becky. "Didn't Roger tell Kevin to meet him at seven tonight? They're probably plotting their next move right now, right next door!"

Now, up until that last part I was feeling a lot better. They had finally figured it out, even what Roddy had told me about Roger sneaking in. But now all four of the ladies were on their feet and headed to the deck stairs. They were going to spy on conniving murderers. This had trouble written all over it.

Twenty-Four

Sheila, Julia, Becky, and Tarrie Ann began crossing the sandy dunes between our house and Roger's, slinking low to avoid being seen, but with Tarrie Ann's margarita glass swishing slightly above head level. From the right angle it looked like the margarita was floating along the top of the dunes. Becky's high heels immediately sunk into the sand. She was dressed to the nines in business attire as usual and reached down to pull her shoes off. She rushed to catch up.

"Ow!"

Becky held her foot up, inspecting the damage from a sharp seashell as everyone froze, hoping the scream hadn't been noticed. The inside lights were on next door, but there didn't seem to be anyone outside on the deck. Those lights were off and nobody approached the doors or windows. Eventually the group began moving again and approached the deck. I followed behind.

"I fought the law and the ..." The ringtone broke the silence. Sheila reached into the back pocket of her shorts as quickly as possible and sent the call to voicemail. Again, the group waited until they were sure they hadn't been heard. They each pulled out their phones and made sure they were set to silent.

"Stay here. I'll take a look," Julia declared. She slowly crept up the wooden steps until she had a good view inside. "They're both here," she whispered back to the group.

"What are they doing?" Becky asked quietly.

"Just sitting at the table. Doesn't look like they're eating. Just talking."

"Can you hear what they're saying?" asked Sheila.

"No." Julia crept back down the stairs. "We're not going to be able to hear anything with the door closed."

"We have to know what they're talking about!" Sheila said, a little too loudly at first. "They may be planning to murder me! Or plant more evidence. Chief Anderson is almost ready to arrest me as it is."

Tarrie Ann, still holding onto the margarita glass, decided to try the side window. She walked around the deck, hunched over but holding the margarita steady with surprising skill, and stood beside a window that was slightly cracked. She motioned back with her free hand, indicating that she could hear a little.

PAW AND ORDER

I had never been so nervous in my life. This was worse than being locked in the cage at the police station. A murderer, or possibly two, was just on the other side of the wall, and these four tipsy ladies were crawling around in the sand trying to eavesdrop. I hopped up onto the deck to keep an eye on the culprits.

My hunting instincts took over, and I began scanning the area. *Yes, I still have hunting instincts—just ask Roddy. I caught him nice and easy.* Sheila kept me fed well with Fancy Feast so I didn't need to hunt, but I stayed active. You never knew when you'd need to call on those skills. Roger and Kevin were at the table, just as Julia said. Outside, all was quiet except for the gentle roar of the waves on the beach. That would cover up a lot of the sounds the ladies might make, but it didn't cover the *clink* of Tarrie Ann's margarita glass hitting the side of the house. Something had crawled by her in the sand, causing her to start.

Roger and Kevin froze. They definitely heard it. Tarrie Ann ducked further down, but there was nowhere she could really hide. Sheila, Julia, and Becky crawled underneath the deck, huddling together like mannequins tossed in a dark storage closet. Becky had arched her torso in a desperate and failing attempt to keep sand off of her business suit, shoes held firmly in her left hand. Julia lay down and quietly started making a sand angel until she noticed how scared Sheila was and put her arm around her.

Roger stood. He walked toward the window. I had to do something. Leaping out to the middle of the deck I pretended to be chasing something, making sure to bump against chairs and the legs of the outdoor table.

It worked! Roger moved to the big glass door that opened onto the deck and looked out. As soon as I knew he saw me, I ran off the far end, landing in the sand and shadows. The door opened. Voices appeared.

"Calm down. It's just a cat," Roger said.

The words 'just a cat' had never sounded so good to me. Sometimes it's to my advantage to be overlooked.

"We wouldn't have to be so jumpy if you hadn't gotten impatient!" Kevin replied.

"Time is running out, Kevin. Mitch was suspicious. He knew I was up to something when I kept offering more money. He found the exceptions in the bylaws, and he was going to confront your mother about it at the party. I had no choice."

The two men walked out onto the deck, Roger looking as smug as ever in his polo and slacks with a pair of golf gloves still hanging out of his back pocket. It seemed to be his signature outfit, even when he wasn't playing. I could see Julia, Sheila, and Becky hiding right below them, trying not to make a sound. A familiar smell reached my nose. Something very faint. So faint that I couldn't quite place it, but I knew it was out of place.

"You didn't have to kill him. I never signed up for that."

"I didn't kill him, remember?" Roger answered. "It was that little lady next door. Her knife. Her fingerprints. She was upset because Mitch was going to get her precious kitty cat kicked out of the community. I didn't even tell you the best part yet. I guess she cut herself, because there was a drop of blood on the handle of the knife. I made sure to wipe it onto Mitch's shirt where they couldn't miss it. They'll match it up to her DNA, and that'll be the smoking gun. She'll have to sell her house, then we'll wrap up the deal for Mitch's and immediately apply for a construction permit. Once we've started legal proceedings, they won't be able to change the rules on us. The all-new Beachside Parrot Eyes Inn will be the hottest property in Florida. You're gonna be rich, Kevin, as long as you take care of your mother."

"Mom is kidding herself, trying to run that old place where it is. It's falling apart, and by the time she dies there won't be anything left for me. She'll be mad, but I'll have everything lined up before she gets a clue."

"Maybe it'll give her a heart attack," Roger joked. "Even easier then!" He pulled out a couple of cigars. "I feel like celebrating!"

Kevin didn't laugh, but he didn't refuse the cigar, either. Roger was the murderer, but Kevin was just as guilty. Greedy and ungrateful. But he was right ... If they found Sheila's blood on the victim, it was case closed. With my cat eyes I could just make out Sheila's face. She was completely shocked that anyone could be so cruel. Fred never talked to her much about his cases. He wanted to protect her from the cruelty of the world. Now that was my job, and I wasn't doing it well enough. We still didn't have any proof that we could give to Chief Anderson.

As the two men enjoyed their cigars Sheila, Julia, and Becky remained frozen in a shadowy mass below their feet. I crept around to where Tarrie Ann was still crouched around the corner of the house. Whatever I smelled before was lost now, covered up by the cigar smoke which was blowing our way in the gentle sea breeze. *Oh, no*, I thought.

"Achoo!"

TWENTY-FIVE

"Who's there?" Roger shouted angrily.

Tarrie Ann walked around the corner, stumbling and waving her margarita glass. "Oh, hiiii, Rog! The moonlight looks good on you!" she said somewhat seductively, but her words were slurring. "I thiiink I had one too many this time. I was looking for Sheila's house."

"It's next door," Roger said, not trying to hide his contempt. "I'll turn on the lights so you can find your way off my property." He reached in the door and flipped the switch.

There was nothing I could do this time. Kevin was looking down, probably to avoid being recognized, and as soon as the lights came on, he saw Sheila, Julia, and Becky through the spaces between the deck boards. "Rog ... we've got a problem," he said slowly.

Roger looked where Kevin was pointing. At first his face lit up a bright red, and I was afraid he was about to attack everyone. But then his anger disappeared and I knew it was worse. He pulled out his phone and spoke to Kevin as he dialed. "Problems are just opportunities in disguise." I could just hear the sound of the phone ringing, then a male voice answering. "Chief Anderson, whoever killed Mitch is trying to kill me, too. Some crazy women are hiding underneath my deck right now! Come arrest them—and bring some help. They won't all fit on your golf cart." He disconnected the call and laughed.

Everyone had come out from under the deck then, and all four women were standing near the corner where Tarrie Ann had been hiding.

"You won't get away with this!" Sheila yelled. "I'm not going to jail for what you did. We all heard you. We'll tell the chief everything when he gets here."

"Tell him whatever you like, lady. I've got you dead to rights, and you can't prove anything you heard unless you were recording us. Which you weren't, were you? I would've seen your phone light up if you'd tried." The looks on their faces told him he was right.

Becky jumped in. "We'll tell Evelyn. Then your scheme will fall apart." She stared at Roger smugly.

"Will you? Really? Because if you do, you'll be signing her death warrant."

Kevin started to say something, but Roger interrupted him.

"Man up, Kevin. If your mom finds out, then you'll get nothing. That stupid deal you got me into in Miami almost ruined us both, but now we're this close to hitting the jackpot. As long as she's clueless, she can stay alive. But if these birds start chirping, she'll have to go."

Kevin hung his head. What a spineless coward he was showing himself to be.

Roger looked back at Sheila. "It's all up to you. You can go to the police and get the old woman killed, or sign the deal I offered you and walk away. I'll even testify that I saw you walk inside as Nancy was leaving to park her golf cart. Your alibi will be back and Evelyn will get to live out whatever life she has left without learning that her son helped murder someone."

"I did no such thing!" Kevin finally spoke up.

"That's not how the law will see it, and you know it. You're an accomplice. It's all the same."

Kevin hung his head again and shut up. At that point, the headlights of Chief Anderson's golf cart pulled into the driveway and all the ladies ran, stumbling in the sand, around the side of the house to meet him. Tarrie Ann still miraculously avoided spilling her margarita. I followed them. Roger and Kevin went through the house and got there first.

"Chief Anderson ... thank you for coming so quickly!" Roger said. As he spoke, another, brighter set of head-lights appeared but pulled into our driveway instead of Roger's.

All of the ladies started yelling at the same time, and Chief Anderson held up his hand. "Quiet! Everybody! That includes you, Roger. We're gonna figger all of this out real soon, so everybody just hold your horses." He looked back at our house where Kojak and Officer Reid had gotten out of their truck and gone to the trash can beside our house. We all stood quietly as they rummaged through the trash.

This was killing me. I had solved the case, but with Fred gone I didn't have anyone who understood me or believed in me. Now, because I hadn't been able to warn Sheila, it had all gone wrong.

Kojak's handler had apparently found what he was looking for. The two of them walked over to the chief who was still holding his hand up, moving it to face anyone who attempted to speak.

"Will this do, Chief?" Officer Reid asked. He held up the coffee cup with the Sea Brews logo. The one Nancy had brought for Sheila the other morning.

"That'll do perfectly, Officer Reid, thank you." Chief Anderson let the officer keep the cup. He looked at Sheila. "Mrs. Mason, if what Nancy told me is true, then this coffee cup should have your DNA in it. I will be comparing that with a spot of blood we found on

Mitch's clothing that wasn't his. If they match up, then I will have all the evidence I need to put you away for his murder since your alibi is now gone. Is there anything you want to tell me?"

Sheila was near tears. She looked over at Roger who grinned and raised an eyebrow as if to ask "What are you going to do?"

I had to do something, but what? Even if I could tell Chief Anderson the truth, he wouldn't believe me any more than he would believe Sheila. But I could tell Kojak! I ran over to where he was standing next to his handler. "Roger planted that evidence!" I told him. "He killed Mitch and set her up. You've gotta help me!"

Kojak looked at me. "What do you want me to do? Where's the evidence? Show me something that proves it and I'll get their attention, but I need proof."

"Quiet, Kojak!" Officer Reid whispered. "Leave that cat alone."

The smell I had noticed earlier was back, and suddenly I realized what it was. "Kojak! Do you smell that?"

"What?" the K-9 whimpered quietly back, trying not to annoy his handler.

"Think back to the dump. The smell they had you looking for!" I pleaded.

"Will you *please* get your cat away from my K-9?" Officer Reid asked Sheila. The 'please' sounded very sarcastic. She reached down and picked me up. I meowed and tapped her hand twice, harder than I intended.

"This is hardly the time for a belly rub, Whiskers," she said. "Still, it may be the last one." Her fingers began scratching against me, sending magical shockwaves of ecstasy throughout my tense body. Helpless again, at the worst possible time. Karen Carpenter's voice in my head was drowning out the talk around me. I forced myself to keep my eyes open.

Kojak's head jerked, and he sniffed loudly. Officer Reid shook his lead and pulled it, trying to keep him quiet and looking nervously at the chief to see if he noticed.

Kojak took off. His handler tried to hold him back, but Kojak was too strong and ran straight at Roger, who jumped back a step. Kojak moved behind him, stuck his nose straight at the seat of Roger's pants. Roger waved him away and turned, but Kojak moved with him, keeping his nose pressed up against the man's butt.

"I'm sorry, Chief," Officer Reid apologized. He ran to his dog and grabbed his collar. Kojak held his ground. "He's alerting, Chief!"

"I can see that," the chief replied. "But *what* is he alerting for?"

That's it! I thought to myself. I had an idea. It was a long shot, but the only one I could think of. I scratched Sheila and she dropped me. Running over to Roger's trash can, I jumped up, grabbed the top, and tried desperately to pull it over. "Help me, Kojak!" I yowled.

There's one more thing dogs are better at than cats—knocking over trash cans. Kojak bolted over, leaped at the can, and it went flying to the ground, spreading trash, and me, all around it. I rummaged through the trash as quickly as I could, praying to Bast, the Egyptian cat goddess. And there it was. In a plastic bag from a grocery store. It was tied up, but I could still smell the evidence. Thank goodness those things always have holes in the bottom! I picked it up in my mouth and carried it triumphantly to Chief Anderson, dropping it at his feet.

"There you are, sir!" I announced proudly. "Proof that Roger murdered Mitch!" I sat straight, holding my collar high where everyone could see and admire my badge. The light from the golf cart headlights made it shine and sparkle.

I waited patiently for my praise and adulation.

"Get this cat out of here!" the chief screamed angrily. "Officer Reid, lock him, and your stupid dog, back in the cages at the police station while I finish arresting this woman! Then clean up this trash!"

"Oh, no you don't!" yelled Tarrie Ann, stepping in front of Sheila. "She's innocent! Roger killed Mitch! He wanted to buy his house, and now he's trying to get Sheila's!"

"That's ridiculous!" Roger yelled. "All the evidence points to her."

"Not the evidence I just found!" I yowled, to no avail. The chief wasn't even going to open the bag. I dodged Officer Reid's half-hearted attempt to grab me, picked up the bag, and took it to Sheila. I tapped her foot twice, then twice more, again and again, willing her to understand. Whether she did or not, I can't be sure, but she reached down, picked up the bag, and opened it. Sheila pulled out two bloody golf gloves, holding them high for everyone to see.

"Those aren't mine! She put those in there to set me up! That's why they were snooping around here tonight!" Roger was on the defensive now and sounded scared. He pulled the other gloves out of his back pocket where Kojak had been alerting. "*These* are my gloves."

The gloves looked very similar, but the smell had given it away.

"Why did your K-9 alert on those gloves?" Sheila asked Officer Reid. "Why would he do that?"

"He must have smelled some evidence. Some smell we told him to look for," he answered.

"Like the smell of a certain person you were searching for recently?" she prodded.

"That would do it," the officer conceded.

Sheila had thought it through and explained it to the chief. "Roger killed Mitch. And afterwards he took Mitch's gloves to replace the ones he got blood all over."

Tarrie Ann, not as tipsy as she had pretended to be earlier, continued the thought. "He stuffed Mitch's body in the trash can knowing it would be picked up the next morning and taken away. But he knew you would eventually search the dump, so he waited to throw away the gloves after you found the body!" She gulped down the rest of her margarita triumphantly.

Roger was sweating profusely now and kept trying to put the blame on Sheila. "Those are lies! It was her knife that killed him!"

"Which you stole from my house after you let Mitch's dog loose to cause a distraction!" Sheila yelled back at him. "I bet that cut on your golf cart seat was from sitting on my knife so that nobody would see it!"

Chief Anderson had been convinced Sheila was guilty, but now he seemed to realize he might be wrong. "I did need to ask you about an unsigned contract from you that Mitch had apparently thrown away, offering more money than you claim he sold to you for. And we found another unsigned contract for Mrs. Mason's house that she also threw away. What are you up to, Roger?"

"Me? I was at the party when Mitch was killed. I couldn't have done it!"

Julia held up a finger and wagged it like the school teacher she was. "Not all the time. Your golf cart was— parked where everyone would see it—but you walked back in the dark, killed Mitch, and snuck into the club-house from the back door."

"Ridiculous! It's *her* blood on the back of his shirt!" Roger blurted out.

"Excuse me?" asked Chief Anderson, staring at Roger. "I never said exactly where the blood was found."

Roger lunged at Sheila, grasping for the bloody gloves that he knew would send him to prison, but Becky stepped between them, jabbing one of her stiletto heels like a dagger against his neck and stopping him in his tracks.

A vibrating noise came from Sheila's back pocket. She pulled her phone out and switched it back from silent to normal.

"I fought the law and the law won."

TWENTY-SIX

Despite the late night, Sheila and I were both up with the sunrise the next morning. It was a beautiful start to the day and felt like a new beginning. The new beginning we had hoped for when we moved down to Paradise Cove. The doorbell never rang, and we just took it easy.

Around midday, she had a treat for me. A catnip ball. I loved those things, but I had made a promise so I picked it up with my mouth and walked to the back door.

"You want to take it outside?" Sheila asked. "It seems you know your way around here now, so okay. Just don't go too far, alright Whiskers?"

I tried to answer, but with the catnip ball in my mouth I couldn't speak. Not that she would have understood, anyway. Maybe she'll catch on one day.

I walked over past Mitch's house to the trail, looking for Zappa. I didn't have to look long.

"Do I smell 'nip?" came a voice from the dunes. Zappa strutted out, moving faster than I had seen him move before. "Well, ain't that somethin," he said. "A copper that keeps his word! Man, that smells good, man!"

I left the catnip with Zappa. It came out of a big bag, so I knew there would be more for me soon. A walk on the beach seemed appropriate, and I headed that way just in time to see Blue fly in and take her spot near the pier. Jimmy wasn't there yet, but he'd be arriving soon, I was sure.

"Hey, Blue!" I meowed. She slowly turned her long neck until she could see me.

"I heard you might not be staying long," she told me.

"Nasty rumors," I replied. "Just settling in. Don't expect to see Roger anytime soon, though."

"Hm."

A bird of few words. I liked Blue, though. And I hoped she'd come to like me, too, once she got to know me. No hurry. We had all the time in the world. I walked down a little way and gave her some space. We both stood in the sand, me watching the waves, her watching for any action below the waves. It was nice, just hanging out quietly. Sometimes you didn't need to speak.

Our quiet moment ended suddenly with the sound of barking. I recognized that voice. Buster! He was pulling

Jimmy down the path, straining to get loose and looking straight at Blue and me. Poor Blue looked confused, seeing the loud, threatening creature with the human who shared his fish with her and Zappa. They would have some adjusting to do. I guessed Jimmy adopted Buster so he wouldn't have to leave. I was starting to feel really bad about suspecting him of being the murderer.

Blue flew away, and it seemed like a good time for me to head home. I could hear Sheila laughing on the deck and saw Tarrie Ann walking out with a pitcher. No surprise she had shown up, apparently with margaritas. As I walked back, Julia and Becky pulled up together on a golf cart.

"I hereby call this meeting of the Paradise Cove Murder Society to order!" Tarrie Ann announced.

"Don't you go asking for trouble!" Sheila scolded her. "I've had enough excitement already. This is supposed to be a quiet retirement!"

Julia picked up a margarita glass and let Tarrie Ann pour her a drink from the pitcher. "You do have to admit, though, we make a great team."

"That we do," added Becky, clicking over to the table in heels of a somewhat more reasonable height. I had wondered if she watered them and they grew overnight. Apparently not. "Chief Anderson owes us one for solving his first murder case." Tarrie Ann filled a glass for her and handed it over.

"And I really owe you all a big one," Sheila said, raising her glass. "To the Paradise Cove Murder Society. You ladies saved me from jail."

"Hello?" I meowed. "What about your favorite feline detective?"

Sheila laughed. "Yes, Detective Whiskers, thank you, too! You really earned your badge last night!"

Did she ...? No, I'm sure she just got lucky for once. I decided to let them enjoy their celebration. I was ready for a nap. I'd missed far too many the last few days. I walked inside, hopped up onto the chair, and then to the shelf with my new pillow from Fred's uniform. Stretching my legs and poking out my claws, I adjusted the material until it was all perfectly comfortable. I curled up into a ball, wrapped my tail around me, and closed my eyes.

"I promised you, Fred. I'll take care of her."

The End

... of book one. Keep reading for a preview of book two.

Other books by the author

The Detective Whiskers Cozy Mystery Series

1 - Paw & Order

2 - CSI: Cat Sleuth Investigation

3 - Miami Mice

4 - Purrder, She Wrote

5 - Mission Impawsible

6 - Only Meowders in the Building

7 - Police Acatdemy

THANK YOU FOR READING PAW & ORDER!

It means the world to me that you have made it to the end of my story ... except it's not the end of the story. It's just the beginning! There are big things in store for Sheila, Whiskers, and all their new friends in Paradise Cove. I've included a preview of the next book here, so keep reading or go ahead and order the full book.

For Sheila, this series will be a journey of rediscovery. She has no regrets about putting her family first, but after forty years of marriage and raising children she's forgotten about so many dreams she had when she was younger. With Fred gone she feels lost. Fortunately, she has new friends who will help push her out of her comfort zone and into an exciting new chapter of life. She's realizing that there is still plenty of life ahead of her.

Whiskers is also at a crossroads. He spent years training as a detective, but he never planned on being without

THANK YOU FOR READING PAW & ORDER!

his partner in crime solving—the one person who actually understood him. With one case successfully closed, is he ready to be the lead detective? And can he eventually connect with Sheila the way he did with Fred?

Remember those delicious dishes from the welcome party at the beginning of the book? I've got the recipes for you! Sheila's Pineapple Salsa, Tarrie Ann's Mango Margarita, Julia's Brownie Mocha Trifle, and Becky's Key Lime Pie—so good that she makes one as a gift for every real estate client and they always give her a great referral! I also got permission from Sandy Scoops to give you an 'easy to make at home' version of their Pineapple Mango Tango ice cream.

Why did I choose to write this series? The world is full of books about young people discovering themselves for the first time. Often, we are told that our lives have a single story. "What are you going to do with your life?" As I get older—I'm in my early fifties now—I'm appreciating more and more that life is a series of stories. They can follow one path or they can follow many paths. I've reinvented my life more than once, and I want to write stories that help my readers see new opportunities for their own stories. It's never too late to take a detour, or a whole new path!

I hope this is just the beginning of our journey together. I'll be writing lots of stories about Detective Whiskers and Sheila in Paradise Cove, as well as other unique characters in other exciting places. Sign up for my newsletter at AuthorChrisAbernathy.com and you'll always

THANK YOU FOR READING PAW & ORDER!

be the first to know when I release a new book or series. I'll also have some special surprises exclusively for my newsletter readers, so get on the list now.

Again, thank you so much for reading this book and keep going for recipes, a preview of the next book, and more!

All of the books in this series will be dedicated to real life cats who have gone above and beyond the call of duty to protect their humans and preserve law and order.

Paw and Order is dedicated to Binky, pet of Cynthia Kootz, who lives in Indianapolis, Indiana. Binky rose to the rescue around midnight one night when a burglar tried to climb in a window of their home. Despite being declawed (don't get me started) Pinky was able to deliver enough pain to the intruder that he left and was later captured by police who noticed his face was bleeding from Binky's bite marks.

Visit my website to read more about Binky's heroism and other cats who saved the day.

AuthorChrisAbernathy.com

Acknowledgments

Writing the Detective Whiskers Cat Cozy Mystery Series has been so much fun. It has also taken a lot of work and help from some amazing people. I want to acknowledge Kelly Utt, Jodi Henley, and Shannon Brown for sharing their expertise in telling and publishing great stories. Craig Martelle, thank you for inspiring so many of us to tell our stories and to create new opportunities for ourselves. My neighbors Mitch and Tarrie have been great sports about allowing me to kill one of them in the very first book and turn the other into a margarita addict. And, of course, my beautiful wife Alice whose greatest gift is encouraging others to become their best selves. She makes me better every day.

Several people have said that they started reading this series because they love the cute covers. That's thanks to the incredible Donna Rogers. You can find her at www.dlrcoverdesigns.com.

RECIPES

Sheila's Pineapple Salsa

When Sheila needed a quick treat to whip up for the welcome party, this immediately came to mind. It's simple, delicious, and always makes you feel like you are enjoying the beach life! It's great served as an appetizer with crackers or tortilla chips (sesame tortilla chips for bonus points!) but it's also an amazing topper for tacos, grilled chicken, or your favorite fish.

All you need is ...

- One whole pineapple
- Two tomatoes
- Two red onions
- One handful of cilantro

Preparation ...

RECIPES

- Cut the pineapple in half, from top to bottom, using a sharp knife (don't let your neighbor run away with it!)
- Starting along the inside of the rind, cut the juicy fruit out, keeping the rind intact. Cut the fruit into small pieces, removing the core.
- Remove the seeds from the tomatoes. Dice what's left. Chop the onions and cilantro.
- Combine the ingredients in a bowl, mix them together, then place the mixture back inside the pineapple rind for a cute presentation.
- Place the dish in your refrigerator for half an hour, allowing the flavors to blend together.

Tarrie Ann's Mango Margarita

No one would ever question Tarrie Ann's expertise when it comes to margaritas, and this mango margarita recipe is her favorite when she wants something extra special. It's a great complement to Sheila's Pineapple Salsa, too!

Ingredients ...

- One cup of ice
- One small mango
- One lime
- One tablespoon of Tajin chili seasoning (available at Latin food stores)
- Three ounces tequila, preferably silver
- Two ounces orange liqueur
- One and a half ounces agave nectar

RECIPES

- Three ounces grapefruit soda

Preparation ...

- Remove the peel and pit from the mango, then puree the fruit in a blender.
- Spread the chili seasoning in a flat dish or rimmer if you have one.
- Slice the lime into wedges. Use one wedge to moisten the rim of your glasses and juice the rest.
- Add lime juice and other ingredients to the mango in the blender. Blend until smooth, then pour into your glasses.

Julia's Brownie Mocha Trifle

Everybody loves a good brownie and they're delicious on their own, but sometimes you need to dress things up a little. And it's hard to go wrong by adding coffee!

Ingredients ...

- A package of fudge brownie mix (sized to fit an 8-inch cooking dish)
- One and three-fourths cups of milk (cold, 2%)
- Two packages of instant pudding mix (3.4-ounce packages)
- A quarter cup of cold-brewed coffee
- Two cups of whipped cream
- One standard size Heath candy bar (crushed)

Preparation ...

- Bake the brownies. Let them cool, then cut them into one-inch squares.
- Add milk and pudding mix (both packages) to a large bowl and beat them together until the mix thickens (about two minutes). Stir in the coffee. Fold in the whipped cream.
- Place a layer of brownie pieces at the bottom of a glass two-quart bowl. Top it with the pudding mix and then the candy bar pieces. Do the same for two more layers of each.
- Place the dessert in the refrigerator until chilled.

Becky's Key Lime Pie

Key lime pie, the official state pie of Florida, is an essential part of the beach experience, as important to adult vacationers as airbrushed T-shirts and shell bracelets are to teenagers on spring break. And the locals love them, too, but if you serve a Key lime pie to a local in Florida, it had better be a good one! Trust Becky. This recipe will make everyone believe you grew up in Key West. And it's easy to make! The homemade graham cracker crust makes a big difference and only takes five minutes.

Ingredients ...

- Graham cracker crust

RECIPES

- One and a half cups of crushed graham crackers
- One-third cup of granulated sugar
- Six tablespoons of melted butter
- Key Lime Filling
- Two 14-ounce cans of sweetened condensed milk
- Four ounces of cream cheese (set it out to soften)
- Three-quarters of a cup of Key lime juice (Key limes are different from regular limes, so make sure you get the right ones—you'll need about twenty)
- Lime zest (two regular limes or four Key limes)
- Whipped Cream Topping
- One cup of heavy whipping cream
- One-quarter cup of powdered sugar
- One-half teaspoon of vanilla extract

Preparation ...

- You'll need the oven warmed up to 350 degrees Fahrenheit for the crust, so get that started.
- Mix all the crust ingredients together in a bowl then pour the mixture into a pie pan and firmly press it into place, including along the sides of the pan at least half way.
- Bake the crust for ten minutes, then remove it from the oven and let it cool.
- Use an electric mixer, if possible, to mix the cream cheese until it is smooth.

RECIPES

- Add the sweetened condensed milk, Key lime juice, and lime zest to the mixing bowl, and mix it again until smooth.
- Pour the mixture into the pie pan over the graham cracker crust.
- Bake at 350 degrees Fahrenheit for ten minutes. Remove it from the oven and allow it to cool to room temperature (about thirty minutes) then refrigerate for at least three hours.
- Prepare the topping by mixing heavy whipping cream in the electric mixer for one minute. Slowly add the powdered sugar and vanilla. Continue beating the mixture until stiff spikes are standing in the bowl. Spread the topping onto the pie and serve.

Pineapple Mango Tango Ice Cream

Sandy Scoops in Paradise Cove is a gourmet ice cream shop, and they use only the freshest ingredients. The actual recipe they use is still secret, but what they gave us is slightly altered to keep their secrets and make it easier to make at home. The results are still an amazing summer treat.

Ingredients ...

- One 14-ounce can of pineapple tidbits (drained)
- One 14-ounce can of diced mangoes (drained)
- Three-quarters of a cup of heavy cream
- A pinch of fine sea salt
- One-quarter cup of sugar

RECIPES

- One teaspoon of lemon juice
- One teaspoon of vanilla

Preparation ...

- Puree it all in a blender until you have a smooth mixture.
- Pour the mixture into an ice cream maker and follow the instructions for the maker.
- Place the ice cream in the freezer until you are ready to enjoy it.

Preview of CSI: Cat Sleuth Investigation

Chapter 1

"...and then you single-handedly chased down the killer, man, knocked him over, and held him at claw point until the police dude arrived with his handcuffs, right, man?"

Zappa rolled his eyes, rolled over on his back, and let the sea breeze gently roll over the hairs on his belly. Apparently, he was tired of hearing me tell him how I caught the man who tried to frame Sheila, my human, for killing our neighbor. Maybe I had brought it up a few too many times over the last few weeks, but the embellishments were his. Mostly. And you gotta admit it was kind of a big deal, solving the first murder ever in Paradise Cove.

Preview of CSI: Cat Sleuth Investigation

The mid-morning sun had warmed the sand and a catnap on the beach did seem like a good idea. I stretched out next to the beach bum hippie cat and closed my eyes. It was a pretty good life he had here, living in the sand dunes. Jimmy still fished on the pier every day and left some of his catch for Zappa and some for Blue, the great blue heron who flew in around lunchtime when Jimmy usually arrived. They'd been worried when Jimmy adopted Buster but the big goofy dog only liked playing with fish, not eating them. So, yeah, sometimes there was dog slobber on their dinner but, hey, beggars can't be choosers, right?

A shadow passed over and the sudden flash of darkness caught my attention. Not Zappa's. He was snoring quietly without a care in the world. I looked over in time to watch Blue gracefully glide down to the sand at the edge of the surf. She was a sight to see with her wings spread wide like that. She landed, pulled her wings in, and stood still like a statue, staring at the water hoping a fish would show up and she could catch lunch for herself. Something without dog slobber on it.

"Hey, Blue." I had left Zappa to nap and walked around the sea oats to chat with Blue. Not that she was a great conversationalist. Our talks were usually one-sided with me offering a monologue until she'd had enough and flew away. "Looks like it's gonna be a pretty day."

PREVIEW OF CSI: CAT SLEUTH INVESTIGATION

Was that a nod? Hard to tell, but I thought I had seen Blue's head move just a fraction. Was she acknowledging me? Probably not. She probably saw a fish.

I took the subtle hint from Zappa's reaction earlier and resisted the urge to update Blue on the latest developments of the case or any other happenings I had observed on my neighborhood patrols. Nothing exciting really. Certainly not compared to a murder and everybody seemed tired of hearing about that already. I just sat in the sand, silently enjoying Blue's company, until a larger wave brought water up to our feet. Blue didn't mind but wet paws were not my favorite thing so I backed up and, making it look like I'd planned to go anyway, walked away.

"Later, Blue," I called back.

Instead of heading back to our house, Sunset Cottage, I decided to take a stroll down the beach. Usually, I saved my long walks on the beach for when Sheila wanted to go but I was in no hurry to get home this morning. A distant "thump-thump-thump" told me that Sheila was still out somewhere. Her grandson, Freddy, had come down from college for a visit. It was his last summer before joining the "real world" and since his Nana, as he called Sheila, now had a cottage on the beach he had chosen to spend the first week or so with her. When she left for some errands this morning he took the opportunity to play his music very loudly. I was certain he'd be hearing from Nosy Nancy, the overenthusiastic HOA

PREVIEW OF CSI: CAT SLEUTH INVESTIGATION

president, real soon. In the meantime, I'd keep my distance and preserve my hearing. A good detective needs to be a great listener.

And I was a good detective. Fred, Sheila's husband and my mentor had trained me well. We'd solved many a case together back in Colorado. Then he died suddenly. Sheila and I were both stunned and lost if I'm being honest. We moved down to the beach, started over, and almost immediately found ourselves thrown into the biggest case of my career. Now, I don't like to brag but I did a pretty good job of developing new contacts, tracking down clues, and delivering justice. Fred would've been proud of me. I kept Sheila safe and put a killer behind bars. I proved that I deserved the shiny badge he had placed on my collar.

I walked past the pier to the end of the beach and turned around. By the time I got close to home the thumping music had stopped. Either Sheila was back or Nancy had come by to enforce the noise limit, I supposed, so it was safe to return. I stuck my head through the pet door Jimmy had helped Sheila install and immediately my nose told me a different story. The pleasing scent of perfume let me know that Susi, the young housecleaner, had come for her weekly visit. Another scent, a less pleasant one, was coming from the guest room. Freddy, in addition to bad taste in music, apparently had an equally bad taste in cologne. And had suddenly decided he needed lots of it when Susi showed up. This was going to be fun. Not.

PREVIEW OF CSI: CAT SLEUTH INVESTIGATION

Chapter 2

"Hi! Sorry about earlier. Nana didn't tell me anybody would be coming."

The wave of body spray that followed Freddy as he came out of his room was overpowering. Glancing through the doorway before it closed I saw a can of something labeled "Axe" on his bed. Susi, God bless her, must have lost some sensitivity to smell thanks to her exposure to cleaning chemicals. That's what I deduced with my finely-tuned detective skills.

"Oh, no worries," Susi replied with a slight giggle. "You must be Freddy. Sheila says you're studying Business in Tallahassee?"

"Uh, yeah. Go Gators!" Freddy stretched his arms out in front of him and moved the right one down, imitating the chomping motion of an alligator as fans do at University of Florida football games.

"More of a Hurricane girl, myself," Susi said, referring to the University of Miami. "Speaking of which, was there a hurricane here that I didn't know about?"

Freddy reached down and picked up a couple of empty soda cans and a large bag of potato chips from the coffee table. "Sorry," he apologized again. "I guess I made myself a little too much at home. Nana spoils me. I'll help you clean up," he said, throwing away the trash and

PREVIEW OF CSI: CAT SLEUTH INVESTIGATION

blushing as he looked at his dirty clothes she was holding.

Susi laughed. "It's okay! It's my job and Sheila's really good to me. You're supposed to be messy on vacation, right?"

"It's not required," Sheila said, walking in the front door with her arms full of groceries. I padded over and rubbed against her leg to say hello.

Freddy stepped over and took the bags from her. "I'll put these away for you Nana." He set the bags on the counter and began pulling out items. One after another he took an item out, looked at it, glanced back and forth between the refrigerator and the pantry then set it down and pulled out another item. Sheila and Susi watched him and laughed.

"Just put the ice cream in the freezer and leave the rest for now," Sheila finally told him. "I'll put everything up in a bit. Susi, can you open the windows? I'll get the fan. It smells like somebody dropped the entire Macy's fragrance counter in here."

I meowed my agreement.

Freddy was blushing again but his face still wasn't as red as my eyes were.

Preview of CSI: Cat Sleuth Investigation

"How long are you staying?" Susi asked, changing the subject while she opened a window and took a deep breath of fresh air.

"Just a week or so," Freddy answered. "I wish I could stay longer but I need to get back and find a job for the summer. Gotta pay for one more year of school before I graduate and build my own business. I'm gonna be a big tycoon!"

"Tycoon of what?" Susi paused between windows and looked at Freddy who looked down and shuffled his feet.

"I, uh, haven't decided that part yet. But I'm gonna be big!"

Sheila and I bit our tongues. Freddy clearly had big dreams. What he did not have, was Rizz. I'm not sure if I used that correctly but based on overhearing the endless stream of TikTok videos he watched it meant "the ability to smooth talk the ladies." Freddy was about as smooth as the pineapple he had just set on the counter.

"Too bad there aren't any jobs in Paradise Cove," Susi offered.

"Yeah, too bad," I thought sarcastically. Sheila and I had settled into a routine and I was looking forward to getting it back in a few days.

PREVIEW OF CSI: CAT SLEUTH INVESTIGATION

"Actually..." Sheila started to say something then stopped herself.

"What's that, Nana?"

She waved it off. "Oh, nothing. Never mind."

Susi pushed the issue. "No, Sheila. What were you going to say?"

"Well," Sheila answered reluctantly, "I just ran into Evelyn from the Parrot Eyes Inn. Her bartender suddenly left without even giving a notice. She's just getting into her busy season and she needs the money from the bar to make a profit. Without it, she may have to close down. I offered to help some but I'm too old to work the hours she needs."

It was Freddy's turn to laugh. "I'd like to see that, Nana! You behind the bar mixing up drinks!"

Sheila looked at him sternly. "I'll have you know, young man, that I was a bartender when I was younger. In fact, that's where I met your grandfather."

"Really?" Freddy was shocked.

"I wasn't always just your Nana, you know. I used to get lots of tips, too. Get a little flirty and those men would spend their whole paycheck on a Friday night."

PREVIEW OF CSI: CAT SLEUTH INVESTIGATION

Freddy put his hands over his ears. I'm not sure I wanted to hear this either but after all these years I'd never heard how she met Fred. I was interested.

Susi was, too, it seemed. "Tell us about when you met your husband," she asked.

Sheila took a deep breath and sighed. She sat down in the recliner and motioned for Susi and Freddy to relax on the sofa. "I fell in love as soon as he walked in the door." She pulled her hand up to her mouth, paused, and closed her eyes tightly. Gradually her eyes lifted and a small smile appeared on her face. "It took him forever."

Freddy and Susi sat silently beside each other. I hopped up to my special pillow on the shelf.

"He wouldn't even come up to the bar. He came in with his friends from the precinct every day after work. They sat at the same table by the wall and took turns buying a round. But when it was Fred's turn to buy he'd hand the money to one of his buddies and make them come to the bar. He was too shy to talk to me but I would always catch him watching me. Every day for about six weeks. Eventually, I got fed up with waiting and walked over to the table."

"What happened?" Susi begged. She was sitting on the edge of the sofa.

PREVIEW OF CSI: CAT SLEUTH INVESTIGATION

"I told him that I wouldn't be working the next night so if he wanted to stare at me he'd have to take me out to dinner. I said I'd be waiting for him when he got off work."

Freddy's jaw dropped.

Susi squealed. "I love it!!! Please tell me he showed up!"

"With a dozen red roses," Sheila said proudly. "He had on a new suit that was a little too long in the arms and his shoes were so shiny I could see my face reflected in them. We went to the fanciest steakhouse in town and it was delicious but neither one of us finished our food. We just talked and talked and talked until they kicked us out at closing time. He told me everything he'd been saving up for six weeks. Six weeks later we were engaged and I quit working so I could be the perfect wife."

"He made you quit working?" Susi asked, suddenly upset.

"He didn't make me, dear. I think he would have been happy no matter what I decided to do. But by that time I'd decided that the only thing I wanted to do was be with him." Sheila smiled and paused a moment as if caught in a good memory. "I certainly didn't want to flirt with other men for tips anymore. I could tell he was good at his job and I trusted him to take care of me. And I took care of him. I know it's not the fashion these days but we were perfect partners. I raised the kids, had his

Preview of CSI: Cat Sleuth Investigation

dinner ready every night, and made sure he never had to worry about anything once he got home."

"I wish I could have met him," Susi said quietly. She looked up at the shelf beside where I was sitting on my pillow. "He looks so handsome in your pictures."

Sheila turned her gaze to Freddy. "You look just like him."

Susi looked at Freddy. "You do! So cute!"

Freddy was blushing yet again.

"Do it, Freddy!" Susi said.

"Do what?" he asked.

"Take the job!" She turned to Sheila. "Can he stay here all summer if Evelyn hires him?"

Oh, no. I could see my peaceful routine disappearing quickly.

"I don't see why not," Sheila answered. "And Evelyn would be thrilled."

"But I don't know anything about being a bartender, Nana," Freddy said. "I've only been 21 for a few months."

PREVIEW OF CSI: CAT SLEUTH INVESTIGATION

Sheila stood up. "Then we don't have any time to lose." Thumbing through some books on the shelf she found one called The Little Black Book of Cocktails. "Lessons begin now!"

Chapter 3

"You've saved my life, Sheila!"

Evelyn was thrilled to hire Freddy.

"He's just beginning," Sheila warned her friend, "but he's catching on quickly. I think he learned more at college than he wants his Nana to know about."

Evelyn took off to the front of the hotel where someone was waiting to check in. The bar wasn't very big. It had half a dozen stools along the railed bar and a half dozen four-top tables spread out around the room. And like the rest of the hotel, it should have been updated a long time ago. The mirrored shelves behind Freddy were a little dusty, too, but the place had some character. I could imagine some well-dressed ladies and gentlemen gathered around having a grand time in better days.

I had to admit that Freddy had impressed me. Not that I had sampled any of his drinks. I don't drink on the job and with Fred gone I'm always on the job protecting Sheila. Of course, I didn't drink before either. A little milk back in the day, nothing harder than that, and just water now. But the customers seemed happy with their

PREVIEW OF CSI: CAT SLEUTH INVESTIGATION

drinks. Other than one sketchy-looking man at the end of the bar who didn't seem happy about anything. His unkempt beard, long hair, and sunglasses stood out in the hotel bar, almost as much as I did. Sheila had insisted I could stay home but I was still a little shocked by the idea of her having been a bartender and wanted to see it for myself so I snuck out the pet door and hopped on the back of the new golf cart she had recently purchased.

Discovering that the Parrot Eyes Inn was a pet-friendly hotel had hurt a little, to be honest. Pretty much every business in Paradise Cove welcomed pets which made me wonder why Fred and Sheila had never brought me down when they came on vacation all those years before. But I guess not many police detectives bring their partners on vacation with their wives so it made sense, kinda.

"I can't stay much longer, Freddy," Sheila said. "Think you'll be alright?"

"Yeah, Nana. If somebody orders something I don't know I can always pull it up on YouTube. Or your book," he said, patting his back pocket where he'd put the book she gave him.

"Or ask Evelyn," Sheila offered. "I know I've seen her back here behind the bar over the years when someone needed a break."

PREVIEW OF CSI: CAT SLEUTH INVESTIGATION

A middle-aged man sat down on a stool and smiled at Sheila. She smiled back. He was holding a small cooler. A ring with a large blue stone stood out against the bright white of the cooler.

Sheila commented on the ring. "That looks like moonstone. Birthstone for June, you've got a birthday next month, am I right?"

"You are," the man replied. "Just don't ask how many it will be." He chuckled.

"What can I get for you, sir?" Freddy asked.

"Old Fashioned for now," the man said. "But I need a big favor. Some old friends are coming into town tomorrow and, I know you don't offer beach service but I'm a good customer and I'm pretty sure Evelyn will say it's okay. There'll be a nice tip in it for you if you can deliver us some drinks before you start your shift."

Freddy looked at Sheila who shrugged. Nobody consulted me which was a good thing because I had no idea what the local law said about alcohol service. One more thing I needed to study up on, just in case.

"I don't mind," Freddy answered eventually. "If Evelyn says it's okay I'll be happy to. Do you want to place the order now or should I bring menus out to the beach tomorrow?"

PREVIEW OF CSI: CAT SLEUTH INVESTIGATION

"Good man!" the customer said, seemingly very pleased that he would be able to look good for his friends. "Bring some menus out for my friends, three of them, but what I want isn't on the menu." He pointed to a framed magazine article on the wall beside one of the tables.

Freddy squinted his eyes and looked. He started to walk around but Sheila stopped him.

"I'll save you a walk," she said. "But it's worth reading the article sometime. He wants the Spanish Moss, correct?"

The man smiled and nodded. "That's the one!"

Freddy reached and pulled out the cocktail book Sheila had given him.

Sheila and the man laughed. "You won't find it in there, son," the man told him. "The Spanish Moss was a one-of-a-kind drink created by a famous bartender as a special gift for the grand opening of the Parrot Eyes Inn. It won the Florida Cocktail of the Year award that year and then they retired it."

"Retired it?" asked Freddy. "If it was so good, why wouldn't they keep serving it?"

"Too much trouble," Sheila said.

PREVIEW OF CSI: CAT SLEUTH INVESTIGATION

Freddy looked like he was having second thoughts.

"Don't worry, son," the man told him. "It's no trouble to make the drink. It's just getting the special ingredient. The Spanish Moss is served with some real Spanish Moss from the branches of a Live Oak tree to give it a unique look."

"You want me to climb a tree, pick some moss, and put it in the drink?" Freddy asked tentatively.

"No need for that," the man said. He opened the cooler he had placed on the bar and took out an ice tray with six cubes of ice. A clump of Spanish Moss was frozen inside each of the cubes. "I've done the hard part for you already. Just pop these in the freezer until it's time to make the drinks."

Freddy looked relieved. "What about the recipe? Is it in the article?" he asked, looking back over to the framed magazine.

"I wish!" said the man. "I've been begging Evelyn for the recipe for years - I even made an offer to buy the Inn but she turned me down. You'll have to get her to help you."

"Well, it seems I've done all the helping I can for the night," Sheila stated. "You've got things under control, Freddy, so I'll take Whiskers home now." She picked up her bag and walked around the end of the bar, making sure to say goodbye to the other man sitting there

PREVIEW OF CSI: CAT SLEUTH INVESTIGATION

quietly. That was one of the lessons she'd taught Freddy. Anyone at the bar deserves your attention, even if they don't want to talk. You still need to make sure they know they are welcome.

"I'll see you at home Freddy," Sheila called back. "And sir, I'll see you and your Spanish Moss at the beach tomorrow. My friends and I will be there catching some rays!"

The gentleman smiled a big smile. "I look forward to it! Walter's my name."

He seemed a little too enthusiastic about that. I would need to keep an eye on them.

"Sheila. See you tomorrow," she said as we walked away.

End of preview

Buy CSI: Cat Sleuth Investigation now!

Printed in Great Britain
by Amazon